The Easy Way Out

BARBARA BAYLEY

2017

ISBN: 1975922514
ISBN 13: 9781975922511

Once to every man and nation comes the moment to decide,
In the strife of truth with falsehood, for the good or evil side. . .
And the choice goes on forever 'twixt that darkness and that light.
James Russell Lowell, 1845.

Mr. Mariposa's Political Ethics class 101, Banana Bay (Florida) High School

Class, settle down, please. Sounds as though you enjoyed your spring vacation. Cell phones on mute and away from your sight. Thank you. . . Caley? What page? No, this is not in your book. Please take notes.

Now then: whatever age we are, at any particular moment in time, we believe ourselves to be oh-so wise and thoughtful and loving; caring of others, generous and honest. Yes, honest to ourselves and to others, so that there is no disconnect between our outside self that others see and the inside private self that we know. Two truths, like two cels of film, sliding one in front of the other so that the outlines match perfectly—the Outside Truthful and Honest Me and the Inside Truthful and Honest Me.

Except.

Except: how honest are we about ourselves, actually?

Here's an example: a three-year-old is caught red-handed up on the kitchen counter with his hand in the cookie jar, and upon seeing his mother, he insists, "This ain't me! *This ain't me!*" (Laughter.) In grownup terms, "I am not a crook!" (Scattered laughter.) Well, anyway. That's a disconnect and of course we expect that kind of disconnect from a preschooler. Not from a President, say.

So what happens if we are not telling the truth *about* ourselves *to* ourselves? It would be like being colorblind, would it not? The colors we tell ourselves that we see would still not be the true colors. We would have to rely on someone who is not colorblind to help us pick out the correct clothing, the best shade of blue car, the non-jarring yellow house paint that we "know", despite everyone else's saying otherwise, in our eyes is gray.

So we would have to trust that the person giving us this advice is being honest and not just foisting on us the worst shades of colors, either out of laziness, or even all the way to envy, vengefulness, vindictiveness, backbiting—we would need a person who has nothing to gain by helping us.

However, *what if* the person we rely on to tell us the truth about colors is *also* colorblind and doesn't even know it? What then?

Oh, *now* I have your interest. All right, class, let's try an experiment. Is there anyone here who is colorblind and willing to admit it? Hands? . . . No? Well, then I'll just tell you all that *I* am colorblind and I'll use myself as--ah, Owen. Good man. Had to process it internally first, didn't you. . . . Come on up front, if you don't mind.

Owen, what kind of--? Ah, red/green. That's the most common variety. Note, class, there *are* other kinds. For today we'll just use red/green colorblindness. That's the one Owen and I share. Otherwise, of course, he and I are perfect. (Laughter.)

Now, Owen, tell me: who chooses your clothes? . . . .Your mother. Your jeans are blue, of course, same as everyone else's in the world. (Laughter.) Your shirt—what color did she tell you it is?

. . . Ah, a beautiful shade of red. Class? (Nods of affirmation.) But to Owen and me it looks—yes, gray. Now, what if I were to tell you, Owen, that your shirt is actually yellow? Yes, see—now I've set up a disconnect. Owen has to choose now to believe either me or his mother, both of us authority figures; and *I'm* the one with the power over his grade. (Laughter.) Not only that, he might start wondering *why* one of us is not telling him the truth and what that person might gain from it, what that person's motivation is.

Serena, yes. . . . Thank you as usual for your concern of others, but no, I'm not picking on Owen, right, Owen? You see he survived. You may sit down. . . . (Hearty applause.) Ah, see? For your honesty and bravery, Owen. You have a roomful of friends. Wouldn't life be wonderful if, every time we were honest, we got a round of applause? (A smattering of half-hearted sarcastic handclaps.)

Truth: tough subject, isn't it? There's truth and there's trust. We trust our political leaders to tell us the truth, but there's a danger here—that *if they are lying to themselves* about what the truth is, then we need to stay extra-vigilant and listen even more critically.

Caley, you've been waving your arm for the longest time. What is your question? . . . .Ah. Not a question, but a comment. Go ahead.

. . . You just don't trust anyone, eh? Not even your best friend Serena? Who then--? Ah, just yourself, ultimately. An interesting response, except that before you could talk as a baby, you were already deciding in a very primitive intuitive way whom you could trust, and if no one, then you would be forced to rely on yourself, which is a rather crazymaking position for a helpless infant to find itself in; and which is precisely why we have caregivers for toddlers who cannot yet reach the remote and click on MSNBC.

. . . Too boring, you say, Caley? What, you just want the easy parts of life? And yet I stand here before this class of juniors and—yes, one enthusiastic senior, I see you, Ashton, you can put your hand down—a round of applause for our token senior, please. (Whistles and applause.) I stand here talking and exhorting you to think, to weigh, to use your unique brain cells, when I could be taking the day off correcting papers, to tell you that critical thinking is difficult—*and necessary.*

. . . Yes, Caley, this possibly will be on the test. And yes, before you start groaning, it *will* be an essay test. To quote Sweeney Agonistes in the T.S. Eliot poem, "I gotta use words when I talk to you." And so do you. So no true/false.

A hand or two before the bell—Serena?. . .Yes, trust in God. I applaud your belief system. We all must come to believe that our lives matter, that there's some purpose in our being here in the first place. And yet, Serena, critical thinking still must come into play or you will have to defend the idea as utter fact that the ark held enough food for all those animals, and Noah and family were not knee-deep in excrement by the third day. (Laughter.)

Ashton, your father's a lawyer--tell us all what "Truth to power" means. . . . Yes, correct. And if we cannot safely speak the hard truths, both positive and negative, to those in power, we are indeed in trouble. If those in power will only hear good things about themselves, they are in the weakened position of being coerced by flattery.

A humorous example of that would be the story of the emperor who wore no clothes. A dangerous example would be—well, to put it in today's terms, it would be if our President, say, relied on positive news briefs *only* about himself, by flatterers who had something to gain--like their paychecks. *Egos unhampered by self-awareness and humility equal dangerous situations.*

Caley, welcome back. I've been watching your eyes glaze over. Here--I'll write on the board what I just said, for you and the class. And spoiler alert: this *will* be on the test.

I'll tell you what: let's make it a take-home test-- give me 300 words about that sentence, with some examples. And bring me in two—no, three-- examples of editorial cartoons that speak truth to power, for extra credit.

. . . Caley, you can download them online or look in the newspaper and magazines. I will not do more of your homework for you than that. Still bored, are you? Well, there's the bell—you may now leave this room of political ideas to join the unexamining crowd in the hall. . . . (Much commotion.)

Caley, hang on a minute. . . . Listen, young woman, you have a brain. I hate to watch you just sliding through school the way you're doing. . . . Yes, I *know* you're in a hurry to meet your friends. I just want you to know that if you need some help with this course. . . all right. Another time.

Hey, Owen—thanks for helping me out. Got a question for me? Caley, before you leave--would you tell Owen and me what color tie I'm wearing today?. . . *Purple.* Ah. Bright purple. My favorite color, although I can't see it quite the same way you do.

Not your favorite color, eh, Caley? Well, that's honest. The more you age, the more I think it will grow on you.

1

JUNE 2017
BANANA BAY MALL, FLORIDA

"Diaphanous"—what a *translucent* kind of word: like a butterfly in the "Avatar" film. "Filmy", like an ephemeral butterfly.

I am standing before a three-way mirror (I wish I had one of these at home) in the dressing room at Macy's in the mall, and I am modeling for myself this absolutely drop-dead gorgeous bikini.

The color is muted and mottled. No, "mottled" is not the right word. Words have to really fit in order to suit me, the way this particular bathing suit out of the half-dozen others I have tried on fits me. Omg, does it *fit* me!

So okay, its color: if you had finger paints and you smoothed the different colors onto paper and then spattered water onto the paints-- *that* is what this would look like. Yes—that's what makes it so terrific. It's almost iridescent. Oh yes, it pleases me.

That, and the fact that this is my first-ever and most expensive two-piece bikini bathing suit that I have yearned to own and I, Caley Marshall, age 17 (halfway to 18), pose and shift back and forth in front of this wonderful three-way mirror, and I look—oh god, I look *spectacular*! When I lean over frontwise I can actually see an indent between my boobs; and see how *spectacular* I look when I check out my *actually cute* rear end, especially when compared to the other girls in my gym class! My staying away from junk drinks and candy bars has really paid off. And look how clear my skin is!

"Hurry up! Let me look! I want to see!" Serena, my very best friend in all this world. I have forced her to sit in one of the dressing rooms with the door closed until I tell her to come out and give me her opinion. But I don't want to share this moment yet. I'm still entranced by the look of my own body—it's curvy where it's supposed to be, and flat in the tummy where it's supposed to be. So it doesn't cover the tiny birthmark just below my Barbie-doll-like waist, but okay. I toss my hair, lightened by the Florida sun, and I make a self-conscious silly face at myself. Oh, god--! add the right pair of sunglasses and maybe a floppy hat--!

"You didn't call me!" Serena shows up behind me in the mirror. She's shorter than me and where we used to be able to wear each other's clothes, she has grown kind of pudgy by refusing to go on the same diet with me and I can't let her strain at any more of my tee shirts and zippers. It's too bad, too, because she has a lot more money than I ever do, to buy new outfits. And her outfits are luscious, but they kind of hang on me now.

We haven't spoken about this out loud, but we're friends, so I know she understands.

"Turn around." She studies me, frowning. "Caley--I don't think your mother will let you wear that. Not to the beach. Not with other people around."

While she says "people", we both know she means "boys". We both know that she means the sexy senior who just graduated a year ahead of us, Ashton Reed, in our school chorus, with the beautiful eyes and the voice so sweet, never cracking, that he gets all the tenor solos when we are assigned new music. Once I turned around to tell him so, but then was too shy. I'm working up the nerve to talk to him. Except all I can think of is jokes like, "How's the weather up there?"

That kind of juvenile stuff.

"Sure she will," I say, but now there's doubt in my voice, where I was so enthusiastic a moment ago and now she's reminding me that he's leaving for a year and I won't see him, maybe *ever* again. "Serena, it's *my* money. I *earned* it."

"Yeah, I know, but". . . .

There is a large un-butterflylike shadow behind me as Serena is moved aside. "She's right. You're not wearing that out in public."

"Doris—it's *my* money! I earned it!"

I watch the lips purse and the frown between my mother's eyes deepen. "You go out like that, you're just advertising yourself."

I redden at that remark. Oh, how can she manage to make everything seem so ugly? *She* leaves our apartment wearing some of the stupidest stuff *I've* ever seen.

"I think I look good," I say in a defensive voice. "And you're *old!* You're —what?—fifty-nine effing years old! What do *you* know about what looks good?" Now we look alike in the mirror, both of us with lips and brows identical, both of us with our chins set. Serena has disappeared, as she always does when my mother and I start battering at each other like rams. If we were male. *Do female rams act the same way?* I wonder.

"I said *no.* And watch your language. When you told me you wanted a new bathing suit, I assumed it would be something sensible. A one-piece." She fingers the tag and whistles. I hate it when my mother whistles. I don't know another mother in the whole world who does that.

"Whoa. Did you get a look at the damned price on this piece of rubber?"

"It's latex. And watch your language."

"Watch *yours,* young lady. This discussion is over. Take it off. I'll be by the door where we came in, over in towels."

"Look," I say desperately, "I can wear a coverup with it."

"Kind of destroys what you want to do, doesn't it—parade yourself around like that."

"No! I--!"

"You wore more when you were a baby in a diaper."

I bring out the biggest gun in my artillery and in my most sarcastic voice: "*You!*—you never even *wanted* a girl! You told me so yourself!"

Good. She moves back a little and catches her breath. She thinks I don't notice that I got in my shot, but I did. I did. "Caley, we are not going to have this same old argument in a dressing room at Macy's." She fingers the tag again. "Size six! Who wears a size *six*, for god's sake? That's a kid size! You'd be pulling at the crotch of that thing all day long."

Now she looks in the mirror, pats at her graying hair, smooths the front of her size sixteen jeans, and points a finger at me. "Five minutes or you walk home. Serena, come on."

Serena, who has been sitting in one of the empty dressing rooms, appears. "Uh, Caley—you want me to wait for you?"

I shake my head no, and the two females, both looking surprisingly alike from the back, walk away from me.

I yank my hair back from my eyes. It's just not fair! She's jealous, is what she is! If Dad were here he'd be applauding me now! If he were here . . . if he were only here.

But he'd never been here. The story I'd been told from babyhood on was that when my father heard that my mother had given birth to a girl, even a special one born on the first of January at 12:01 am in the year 2000, he'd fled Banana Bay and nobody had seen him since. *One look,* my mother Doris told me over and over as a story to accompany my potty training, as a bedtime lullaby, as an accompaniment to my nightly meal. *One look and he was gone! A hundred bucks and some baby diapers I got as an award for first baby of the New Year, and it turned out to be a trade: you for him!*

"Our picture in the paper, anyway." I always hoped this would smooth things over. At least she had framed and hung the photo on the wall wherever we lived.

A shadow again behind me. "My vote may not count for anything, but I do think you look quite nice."

I look up. An old woman moves to my right shoulder. We look into the mirror together. "Yes—quite—*diaphanous,* wouldn't you say."

She's gotta be at least 100 years old, I think, and I burst into tears, surprising myself. She pulls a tissue out of nowhere and hands it to me. Her fingers are gnarled and her skin is stained with dark spots—discolored areas, not moles. I peek at her while I'm blowing my nose; I am surprised to see her nose is smooth—I had almost expected a big wart at the end of it.

"You know what we two look like?" She smiles and wrinkles appear at the corners of her eyes, like she's spent a lifetime being amused at stuff. (I plan on being a writer when I graduate from college, so I notice things like that. I'm going to write a best-selling novel and make a million dollars with my first book.)

"Good luck with that. Anyway, we make an interesting couple: you're Cinderella and I'm your fairy godmother, about to grant you a wish."

"I'd look pretty funny going to a ball in a bathing suit," I choke the words out and try to smile back. I'm thinking, *we look more like Before and After.*

"Guess I'd be After. Well, you know, *I* was just feeling very sorry for myself, looking at bathing suits for older women. I never realized until I tried one on that I had such ropey-looking legs. And I never believed my chest would go all the way to my waist—not that I even have a waist anymore. Hard to believe I once looked like you. Well, something like you."

I *really* don't want to hear that she once (*maybe centuries ago when dinosaurs roamed the earth—I'll have to remember to tell this to Serena*) looked like me, and I'm not that crazy about having to look at her body right now, either. She is wearing a bright purple bathing suit, the kind with a little skirt attached to it, and she looks quite ludicrous. Above the square neckline her saggy skin wrinkles and puckers like a crumpled paper bag.

"Yes, I never appreciated my own body when I was young, and now it's maybe too late," she muses, squinting at the mirror. She runs a hand through her short wiry white hair and I flinch at the flap of flesh dangling beneath her upper arm. "I just wanted life to be easy and fun, like you. You know—skip over the tough parts, like you do in Poly Ethics class. Be the class clown. Nothing wrong with being amusing, of course. I love a good joke myself."

"Did—did I have you as a sub? Is that where you know me from?" I've never seen any of my teachers undressed like this, so it *could* be someone who subbed for just a day. Even our gym teacher wears more clothes than a bathing suit, and she has a nice firm figure.

"Life. It's such a peculiarity of life—it can only be lived forward, and yet can only be understood when we look backward."

"Backward! Why would anyone want to look *backward*? I could hardly wait to stop being a little kid and now I can hardly wait until I'm grown up and out of my mother's life! *And dammit I deserve this bathing suit!*"

I blink. I've never said those baby-stamping-her-foot words out loud, and I've just said them to an old lady, a total stranger to me, as we stand in the deserted narrow hallway of a Macy's dressing area, both of us nearly naked. I read a story once about how strangers on an airplane confessed things to their fellow passengers, dirty secrets they would never tell anyone they knew, just because they believed they would never see these people again—and then the plane crashed on a deserted island and they were marooned with all these same people who knew all the awful stuff they had ever done. . .

I am suddenly uncomfortable. "Uh—excuse me, please, but I have to. . . ."

"When your mother—you call her Doris, I gather -- says five minutes, she means it, doesn't she? I'll bet this Doris has driven off without you more than once, just to teach you a lesson."

"Yeah, she's kind of peculiar that way. How did you know?"

"I study voices. I can tell a person's personality and character from the tone of the voice alone. Take yours, for example. I can tell just what you're going to be like in life, from your voice."

Her voice is soothing and gentle, I notice now. It's kind of like a cat's contented purr. I feel myself calm down. I just don't want to look at her, because the figure and face are at such odds with the sound.

Then to my chagrin (a word I've never used before, but it pops into my head as the correct one here) I don't know why, but I start crying again. "I just wish I could grow up fast! Not live under her roof any more. 'As long as you're under my roof you'll abide by my rules, young lady!' "

"That was very good. You have her voice down pat."

Now I stare at her. "I *do* study voices, as I said. You would do well on a platform, you know. It's no wonder you're the class clown." She points a wizened finger at me.

Where did that word come from? I've never used it before.

" 'Wizened' --sounds so much like 'wizard', doesn't it? Always makes me think of that scared little man behind the screen in the Emerald City. Now—you need to change and meet your mother Doris before your five minutes are up." She examines her crabbed fingers with humor.

Five minutes! I feel as though I've been standing here for hours. I blink. It's like I've been hypnotized. *What a weird sensation, but not unpleasant.*

"Believe me, you'll get used to it."

Did she just say something? Did I imagine it?

"Well . . ." I pluck at the bathing suit and she nods. I feel a little dizzy and confused as to which room is mine. "That one," says the old woman, again pointing. "You'll have enough time. I guarantee it. Time is such an *elastic* sort of thing, isn't it? A minute can last an hour and an hour feel like the blink of an eye. Einstein used to explain relativity that way—when you're kissing someone you love, like Ashton, no matter how long you kiss, it can feel like no time at all, and when you're sitting on a hot stove, a second can feel like an hour. Of course, I take his word for it; I've never actually sat on a hot stove."

If I had been paying attention I would have heard the word "Ashton" and I would have questioned her, questioned her critically, as Mr. Mariposa is fond of saying, since I have never been alone with Ashton, let alone kissed him. But I have tuned the old lady out. I've found my shorts and my top and have yanked them on, leaving my coveted bathing suit in a tired-looking little heap on the floor.

"And who would we be if we never coveted something or someone? Are we nothing but mirrors, reflected in someone else's gaze? Do we even exist if no one is noticing us?"

"Uh—did you say something?"

"I said I'll hang the suit back up for you so you can get going."

"Thanks, but—so, do you work here?" I come out of the dressing room and I can't help it: I take an involuntary breath, looking at that terrible purple bathing suit she is wearing. It's like a car wreck that you can't stop staring at, after you've made sure you don't know any of the people involved. There's even a large artificial purple flower at what would be the waist.

She laughs. "Would you believe *I'm* still a comic, at my age?" She strikes a pose by putting a hand over the flower, the other hand against her bony clavicle, and points her feet at an angle. "Oh yes, I too have quite a sense of humor. Actually, that's what got me where I am today." She looks up to the ceiling as if she's expecting an answer from there, then seems to fall into a daydream. I've seen old people do that—kind of nod off while they're still talking.

That's odd, I now notice: she's barefoot and her toenails are painted the *exact* same shade of purple as the tacky bathing suit. I'm not at all color-blind. In fact, I think I have extra-sharp color sense. It's not unusual that both Mr. Mariposa and that nerd Owen can't see red and green. Males have a higher incidence of that genetic glitch than females.

"Oh my God. You closed the Crack? Then You must want—ah. Yes, of course." *She's nattering on just like an old fossil,* I think.

"And which one of us is daydreaming, Caley—you or me?"

She knows my name! She *must* be a substitute teacher. Or she heard Doris say it. She's a sharper old lady than I gave her credit for.

She then stoops carefully while I avert my eyes—I don't need a glimpse of her corrugated rear end, even in that skirt. "Bad back, you know. No, you don't know, do you? But you will, in time," and picks up my discarded suit. "Still warm from you. That's a *major* help. I'll take your used tissue as well. Ah, good. Now—it's as though you were never here, isn't it?" She laughs, showing a set of surprisingly chalk-white teeth, and then peers down at the carpet and sighs. "I would have thought girls your age would bite their nails. Or brush out their hair. You know, leave some extra work-able residue. Ah, well."

But I have fled to the door near the towels, where I find no mother or friend. They *have* left without me! But there's Serena outside the glass doors frantically waving to me and now I see Doris sitting in the car with the engine running and I'm sure the AC is on full-blast to get rid of her cigarette smoke. She looks grim, which means the radio is on—the news again. Honestly, the news—blah, blah, blah. Lately it's been keeping her in a very bad mood. Yeah, well, I don't care if she *is* in a bad mood. I am too and I can match her tone for tone, even with Serena sitting next to me and punching at me a little to shut up.

Maybe *because* Serena is sitting next to me in the car, which smells, as usual, of smoke. Why can't our car smell like Serena's parents'—new and leathery? Why does my life have to be controlled by a neurotic menopausal woman who spends any extra money we have on Winstons?

"I hate my life," I snort.

"Yeah, well join the club, kid. *I* hate your life, too."

"That's *not* what I--!"

"Drop it. Just drop it. Get me any madder and I'll drive this thing right off the causeway bridge into Banana Bay—and don't you *dare* lecture me that it's 'not a bay or a river, it's an estuary' !"

Serena squeezes my arm. "We've been listening to the news," she whispers.

"That damned crazy President! Five months in office and he's already signed a bill to have his face carved into Mt. Rushmore! I'll tell you what he needs to have carved there—his *butt!* Ruining our national parks, letting crap from factories flow into our rivers, telling everyone that if they don't speak good English they'll be deported—you think *you* speak good English?" she yells to the radio, as though the President can hear her. "You can't even put two coherent sentences together!"

I'd be embarrassed for Serena, except she's been hearing this from my mother since before the inauguration. I don't know what all the fuss is about—to me, one President is the same as another. It's not like I could have voted for him.

She and I sit beside each other in the back seat. The front passenger seat is loaded down with a banker's boxful of envelopes and ledgers. Doris does bookkeeping and bill-paying for a bunch of the local businesses. Other people seem to think she's smart, which infuriates me, because she sure doesn't show it around me. She works from our apartment, which is why I have to be quiet when I come home from school and can't even turn on the stereo or tv. And she tells me that if I want earphones I can buy my own. "*It's my place, too!*" I yell at her, stomping my way to my room, slamming my door.

"Good! Then you pay the rent!" You'd figure she could come up with a better line.

Thinking about that, I'm mad all over again, fuming about how I've grown up with the odor of bitter boiled-over coffee and cigarette smoke and burnt toasted cheese sandwiches, the stench reaching even into my clothes.

("Whoa! You *smoke*, Caley?" This from Tiffany, one of the cheerleaders, a year older than me, in Ashton's senior class. She has me cornered against a wall near the lockers. I'm not scared of her, but she makes my stomach knot, even so.

"So-o bad for you," adds Misty, her ever-present sidekick. They are both beautiful and always so well-dressed, even in shorts and sleeveless shirts. They must spend hours on their hair.

"Sor-ry. Guess we need to move away from *you*. Can't let all that smoke get in our *hair*.")

How do I answer that? How the hell do I explain my mother Doris to anyone?

(Oh god: does *Ashton* think I smoke? When he stands behind me on the risers, is he inhaling *Doris*?) The thought weakens my knees.

"—and listen, missy, when we get home, don't even think of using the bathroom first. I don't know what got to me at lunch, but—"

I slink down in my seat and squeeze my eyes shut. Serena nudges me. "Too much information, Mrs. Marshall!" she laughs, and so Doris does, too. "Serena, you crack me up. I bet you two were switched at birth and I got the wrong daughter!"

I wish. I just wish.

Without warning my mother stands on the brakes. Her box of paperwork crashes against the dashboard. Serena and I jolt against the back of the front seat.

"Jesus, oh my God, Mrs. Marshall!"

"I *saw* her, Serena, I *saw* her!" my mother shouts. "Are you two okay? You had on your seatbelts, right?"

I prod my mother's shoulder. "What happened?"

"Old lady in a purple dress."

"I thought you were going to drive right *into* her!" Serena gasps. "Oh, I'm so sorry for using the Lord's name in vain! Oh, my heart is going a mile a minute! Mrs. Marshall, weren't you *scared?*"

"Me? Nah. Just wanted a closer look at her, that's all!" But I can hear in my mother's unsteady voice that she is shaken. "Get *that*, girls. That old nursing home reject just came outta *nowhere!*"

I turn around and stare out the rear window, but see no one. Purple— something I need to remember about that color—well, gone. That's how thoughts are.

It's a good thing Doris is mostly a pretty good driver. I'll give her that.

3

JUNE 2017

At home I go to my room to sulk. Doris has driven off on some business errand. Serena tried a couple of times to get me to lighten up by squeezing my hand; but when that didn't work, she was more than ready to be dropped off and away from the tension in the car, although you would think she'd be used to it. Over the eleven years (most of our lives, when I count back) that we've known each other she's witnessed many examples of my mother's and my disagreements.

The first time she heard Doris swear at me, she had burst into tears and her body had actually shaken, visibly enough that my mother and I stopped shouting at the same moment. "See, in my family we're Christians and we just don't talk to each other like that," she had told me later, after my mother had grabbed her purse and stormed away in the car, kicking up sand.

I couldn't believe it—I'd *never* been intimidated by Doris, no matter what words she used. "She's just that way," I said. "She makes me so mad! I wish I had a young mother like yours. Mine's already old enough to be a grandma."

Serena nodded. She was always ready to agree with me about anything—that was one of the things that made her such a good friend. "I was ready to *die*. I *would* have, if she'd talked to me like that!"

"Nah. For her that's just for me. For her that's just normal." But I mused, *that's true: Doris does know how to behave herself—just with other people, never with me.*

"No! Uh uh. Parents don't use swear words at their own kids. And what did you mean, telling her you knew she never wanted a girl? Excuse me, but that was just downright—ugly!"

Oh, I loved Serena at that moment for being her and letting me get away with saying anything I wanted. We'd been best friends since first grade when we both got perfect marks on a spelling test and nobody else did, so we had to split the prize—a Hershey bar. That's when we became good-natured competitors, vying with each other for prizes and A's on our report cards. I don't know if I would have done so well if I hadn't had her to push against.

I read once about a racehorse that was kind of lazy, except that his jockey figured out that the horse hated to see another horse's rear end; so the lazy horse ("Seabiscuit", *that* was his name—I knew I'd remember it) pushed himself to always be in front, not facing some other horse's buttocks. That's what Serena and I were to each other—each other's rear end. We loved the idea and would shout at each other, "Rear end!" when one of us did better than the other. It was our private joke.

"From when I could understand words, Doris would tell me she never wanted a girl. I just thought it went along with her cursing, and I figured out that *she* didn't like being a girl, maybe."

"Well, that's just mean. My mother says girls are special."

"So let's trade mothers!"

I liked Serena's mother, short and round, slow-moving and gentle, giving me pats on the back and cushiony surprise hugs. I'd invent reasons to come into their kitchen—a glass of water, a silly joke to tell her—because I knew I could count on a smile and a hug.

I liked their old house, rambling, full of comfortable rooms. I would marvel at all the crosses on the walls. I didn't get it. If their Jesus had died such an awful death, why would they want reminders of it all over the place? What if Jesus had been shot or stabbed to death? Would they have hung replicas of *guns* or *knives* instead?

It was all too confusing to me, even when Serena tried to explain it to me. And I liked her father, although I was wary around him. It was like visiting a foreign country to even say hello to him, his voice was so deep and rumbly. He smelled of earth and tobacco, mystery, uncharted territory, even from many feet away. When Serena would climb, without permission even, onto her father's lap, I would feel a lump rise in my throat.

"Trade mothers? No way!" and Serena bounced so hard on my twin bed that my old metal headboard hit the wall and the little book shelf I'd nailed up fell down.

"Caley! Look at that! That could have fallen down at night and it could have *killed* you!"

We reveled in that idea for a moment, both of us enjoying the drama, Serena's eyes large. "You need to use screws, did you know that? Not nails."

"How do *you* know?"

"My dad showed me." I was stung that she had such easy access to this kind of knowledge, so that I was forced to feel, for the moment, like the rear end of a horse.

"Well--who cares, anyway? That's not what's gonna get me. I'm going to be very, very old when I die."

"Oh Caley, how can you possibly know that? For me, *I'm* going to fall off a beautiful coal-black stallion I've been riding and my lover will pick up my poor throbbing body in his arms and kiss me as I breathe my last breath. His tears will fall onto my ashen face. . ."

"You'd never get up on a stallion—you're afraid of heights."

"Who says? Anyway, it's better than you getting killed by a falling bookshelf!"

"For me," I said, stretching out beside her and pushing at her a little for more room, "I'm going to be very old, and then I will find out that I have a terminal illness—but one with no pain or disfigurement."

"Ooh—good word!"

"Uh huh. And I plan to write on a piece of paper, 'You are not to blame—I chose to end it this way,' and then I'll fold it and put it in my pocket—"

"Gonna sign it?"

"Oh! Forgot that part. Yes, of course, sign it and I'd better date it, too—and then I'll walk out in traffic in front of a big truck. The last thing I'll see in this world will be his trucker eyes huge in astonishment. Maybe I'll have time to wave at him. But it will be sudden."

"Then you'll go right to heaven."

"I don't believe in heaven. Doris says that's for people who have nothing else to believe in and are too self-centered to think that when their lives are over here on earth, they're over."

"That's crazy. Of course there's heaven. Otherwise, why ever do anything nice for anyone? Jesus died for you, you know."

"Well—*I* never asked him to." This was part of what didn't make sense about her religion—someone who didn't even *know* me going through an awful thing like that and then trying to make me be responsible. *And* two thousand years before I was even born. Huh. I wanted to tell Serena, "*He* should have written a note telling me I wasn't to blame," but I was certain I'd get a churchy lecture from her.

"And besides that, Caley, there's a flaw in your story about dying, and it's sexist to boot."

"Oh yeah—what?"

"What if the truck driver is a *woman?* How about if she's a woman who looks like your *mother?*"

I hadn't thought about that. It *was* sexist. And suddenly there appeared in my mind a vision of my mother in a huge semi-trailer, barreling down on me deliberately, being in charge of my end as she was of my beginning, like—like God! if I believed in God.

"Caley, you just shuddered."

"C'mon. Let's go see what kind of soda we have before she gets back." Even with just the two of us, our tiny apartment still seemed full of my mother's presence.

Ten. Serena and I were ten, in Mrs. Hornsby's fifth grade class, in Banana Bay Elementary School, when we split that Coke, chugging it fast before we could get caught, burping in cheerful competition like boys, hiding the can far down in the trash so Doris wouldn't find it. Such a vivid memory, like it happened just yesterday.

4

JUNE 2017

Now, alone, I push my face into my pillow and sob, letting myself be as loud as I want. I cry for having such a hateful mother, for having an absent father who might even be dead by now—I could even bump into him on the street and not know who he is!—and this, as always, makes me cry harder. Even picturing Mr. Mariposa as maybe my father, who will someday turn to me after class and say, "Let me tell you who I truly am, Caley". . . doesn't help this time. *I wanted that bathing suit!*

After a while, as the sky outside my window darkens to mauve and I wonder once more, as I have since I was very young, if Doris will ever be coming back—all *my* fault, she's told me over and over if she doesn't, leaving the tiny me panting in terror over how will I take care of myself alone, me who can't even reach the refrigerator door handle to get food for myself, the tiny me who will put up with all her yelling if only she will stay here, stay home and please, please fix me a sandwich, a glass of milk, it has to be suppertime by now, please don't desert me!

--except this time, *no*! I'm not that little kid anymore! *My* own self, *my* own body, *my* own babysitting money, *my* own life, not hers!

Maybe I should just take my babysitting money and run away. Anything would be better than staying here with a mother who frowns at me, yells at me when she's mad about anything, and despises me for being in her territory.

An old profound sense of being abandoned overwhelms me, an emotion so throat-tightening that if I were not so exhausted from crying, I would go search in my mother's bedroom for any pills she has hidden, and take them all. I wouldn't care what they are—I just don't want to be here anymore. Let her find me dead—that would show her!

Serena crying at my funeral, her parents mourning too, while Doris sits, arms crossed, frowning, refusing to cry—"What's there to cry about? Life's hard and then you're gone." Then Mr. Mariposa shows up at the funeral home, saying, "Oh no! It's too late to tell her". . . Maybe she wouldn't even be there. Maybe she'd just be packing up her old car, ready to leave, free as the breeze without me—"If I didn't have you hanging on me all the time, I could be free as the breeze." Well, I'd be dead and she'd be back to being on her own. No more weight of a kid holding her stuck any more. Maybe, with me gone, my Dad (it *would* be nice if it could be Mr. Mariposa, there's something so kind about him) would come back. Not that I can picture Doris and him together. Yuck.

So who could my Dad be? This thought makes me cry some more. He must really have hated me, to leave as soon as he found out I was a girl. What's so god-damned great about having a son, anyway?

Then oddly, I think of Ashton. Ashton who smiles at me in chorus. I stand (no, *stood*—he's probably gone by now) right in front of him when we line up to sing and his glorious voice makes me want to sing better and I smile at the same time, so that Ms. Watson, the music director, smiles back. Ashton, tall and slim, who loves science and law and that stupid poly ethics course we took together and—*huh*. I stop; that's all I know about him. And now he's in Europe someplace. I didn't pay attention when he told people where he was going, I was so miserable about him leaving, and afraid he'd notice how miserable I was.

But I know what he sounds like and I know what his grin looks like and I know how he looked right into my eyes when he told me, "Good morning," and how I could get down from the risers by myself, but he was always there to help me down, his hand on my arm, keeping it there just a little longer than he needed to. Because he was a year ahead of me, the girls in his homeroom always frowned at me when he paid me just that little bit of attention, and he graduated last month and I'll never see him again, never, ever. Ever—

I sigh and force open my eyes, painfully puffy from crying, and look above my head at the two holes in the wall where I had once so proudly nailed my bookshelf. The wallboard has a gouged, raw appearance. I need to fix the holes, but how? So *much* I don't know, things that other people take for granted, things that *good* parents teach their kids—

--it's just holes in the wall. Ashton would know how to fix it, I'm sure. Again a feeling of missing him overtakes me, along with a wave of hopelessness; so *much* to have to learn! Maybe I should take most of my bathing suit money and buy some paint for the walls—they've been the same yucky shade of yellow since we moved in years ago.

Night after night when I go to bed, ever since I read the story, it reminds me of "The Yellow Wallpaper", about a woman who was confined by her husband and doctor to a single room until she overcame her depression, which meant in those days until she became obedient and subservient. Which meant in those days subduing any passionate sexual feelings she had.

I'll bet she didn't have any after her husband finally let her out of the room.

Could adults possibly have passionate needs? I've tried to picture my overweight mother driving off to meet a boyfriend, whoever that might be. He would be overweight, too, and with a curly wiry beard full of beer foam. They would be in a bar, shouting four-letter effing words back and forth that would pass as love, while deafening music from a jukebox drowned out their voices.

Yuck. Who would want her? And if someone did, wouldn't she then, in love, come home a much nicer, kind of --I don't know, *smoother*—person?

I can't stand to look at those holes and that yellow color one more second. I'm angry and depressed and too tired to want to think about anything. The sky outside is a deeper shade of purple now and it reminds me vaguely of something I saw earlier today. Or last month, maybe. My chest hurts from crying and I'd like to get up for a drink of water and put a cool damp washcloth over my eyes; but my body feels as though it's on another planet, one with so much gravity that I'm sinking, sinking, pulled down through my mattress, down toward the core of the planet's massive earth, and the weight of me is so ponderous that with a few more sobbing shudders I close my eyes and sleep.

5

JUNE 2022
BANANA BAY COLLEGE

There is someone in my room.

My heart is beating so hard I think it will burst out of my skin. The only thing that calms me is that I can smell a familiar perfume: Chanel. The only one I know who wears it is Serena, the only one of my few friends who can afford it.

"She's finally awake!" Someone leans down and kisses me on my mouth and in surprise my eyelids fly open. Ashton! So close to me, breathing on my face, that familiar smile. But *his* face has changed. It looks a little older somehow.

"How—? Ashton, how did you get in here?" My mother would never have let him come to my bedroom. She is too embarrassed about how cluttered I keep it. Besides—her let a boy into my room even if it was neat and my clothes were picked up? Never.

"Caley. Where the hell did you go last night? You missed our graduation party."

"Yeah, where were you?" Serena—I think it's Serena—pulls me up to sit and when she lets go I plop as if boneless, backward again. "Whoa! Caley--you'd better take it easy."

I blink up at my ceiling. This is not my waterstained ceiling.

"What are you two doing here?"

The two people on my bed frown at each other. "When did you finally get home? I fell asleep waiting for you. Oh, Ashton, she looks terrible! Caley, honey, just look at you! Um-- your eyes look a little jumpy. Oh, no--Ash, maybe she's had a concussion or something!"

Now Ashton takes his hands and feels around my scalp. His hands feel delicious and I want to hang onto this moment, peculiar as it is. "Nope. Looks like she just had some totally weird night."

"Without *us*? Shame on her! Maybe she needs some water. You want some water, honey?" this woman shouts at me as though I am deaf. "And a mirror? No, maybe she shouldn't look at herself yet. Caley, you look like a horse ran over you and then a couple of mules kicked you. I'm not trying to scare you, but—I've *never* seen you look this bad. You couldn't have had that much to drink at the beach, though. Ash, what do you think she had to drink?"

I can hear water running, but it's not from the direction of the bathroom. Ashton sits down on the edge of my bed, raises my head and puts a glass to my mouth. The water goes down my throat and I gulp, wanting more.

"Here. I don't know if I should do this, but—oh, Caley!" The woman wails sympathetically. What must I look like? They are scaring me now. And what are they doing in my room? And how did Serena—if that's who she is—lose weight overnight?

"Here, honey. Look at yourself. Let me make you up." A plastic handle is placed in my hand and I look into the mirror.

A me, but not-me looks back. "Hah-h-h!" I scream, dropping the mirror. The person I have seen has lost plumpness in her cheeks and her eyes look less innocent than mine, for some reason, although they're the correct color, as is my hair—but *where is all my hair?* This is a very short cut! "Where has my hair gone?"

"Told you, right?"

"Did you two cut my hair as a joke?" A distressing thought takes hold: I have had a brain operation and cannot remember anything. The doctors had to shave my head and my hair is now just growing back. But that would have had to have been at least six months ago! Have I been in a coma for *six months?*

Ashton and Serena laugh and I take a long look at them. Serena-- slimmed down and grown sleeker. How can that be? Overnight? If that's really Serena.

"You had it cut that way and then you came back and showed us. You told us that we wouldn't have let you do it otherwise."

"Actually, I think it's rather flattering," says Ashton, rumpling my hair in a very casual yet possessive way and getting up with the empty glass. "Want more?"

"But I—I'm *old!*"

"We're all old now, Caley. That's what graduation does to a person." The woman (who might be a trained impressionist made up to look like Serena—I am proud of myself for having that idea) takes the hand mirror from me and studies her own face approvingly.

"How—how did you lose all that weight? I mean, how did you lose it so fast?" My voice sounds different to me now that I've had some water. It sounds—deeper. More an alto than a soprano.

I move my hand to my face and notice that I'm wearing a ring. I turn my hand—I've never done my nails this way -- to look at it. It's a small diamond. "This is new." I've never owned a ring like this. What odd trick are they playing on me?

They both laugh. "You're right—it *is* new."

"Well, at least you remember getting engaged right after the gradua- tion ceremony. We all thought it was so romantic—Ash going down on one knee and singing to you. He surprised all of us!"

"But I can't be engaged—I'm not even 18 yet!"

Now the two people in my bedroom stop smiling. Ashton turns away from me to talk to the woman. "Serena, okay, I know Caley clowns around a lot, but this isn't funny. Something happened to her last night while she was at the other end of the beach, away from all of us." He talks just like a doctor discussing a patient and I give him a frustrated nudge away from me. They both need to shut up and let me think—something is very wrong here!

Serena, a beautiful good-smelling Serena, but not (*she might be; she's confusing me*) the old best friend I know, puts her face close to mine. "Did you meet anyone on the beach last night, Caley? Did anyone give you something strange to drink? Or pills of any kind?" To Ashton she says, "I don't think she'd be that foolish. And we know she doesn't smoke or even like to drink." He nods.

"No—I don't think so—no. You and I and Doris went to Macy's and came home. I lay down and when I woke up you two were here." Now I notice the sunlight. "I must have slept all night!" I feel disoriented as I struggle to sit up. My body is—different: that of an adult, not my adolescent one. "Huh—maybe you're right. Maybe someone gave me something to drink. It's messed up my head."

I study the room for the first time since waking up. There are two beds here instead of one, and someone has come in during the night and painted a walls a soft green color. I peer at the wall over my bed. The headboard has gone and the nail holes have been covered by a print—I recognize it as a Modigliani. So if I know *that*, then I'm pretty sure my brain's not fried. So what kind of not-at-all-funny stunt are these two playing on me?

"Which one of you painted the walls?"

Ashton and Serena watch me, their eyes full of compassion, not amusement. So this may not be a joke, unless they are both accomplished actors. Unless there's a camera hidden in the room and everyone is going to pop out at any moment and yell, "Surprise!"

That has to be it, assuming they're not trying to drive me crazy. Still, I can't believe I've misjudged Ashton as someone mean. And *then* Doris will pop in and laugh her head off at me. Well, I'm not going to give her that satisfaction! Okay—I'll go along.

"What—what did we graduate from?" I ask, trying to sound casual until they trip themselves up.

"Caley, quit it. This isn't a game anymore," Ashton says. "If you're going to keep on like this and not tell us what happened to you last night, I'm leaving. I still have packing to do."

"No, Ash, something crazy must happened and we have to help her. Look, honey, look here--here's your diploma. See? There's your name and everything. Now you just rest until whatever you took gets out of your system."

"There's no date on this diploma." *Hah! I've got them!*

"Yeah, printer's error. They said we could take them back to the office and get new ones. But I kind of like it this way—it makes us ageless," Ashton tells me.

"We'll never grow old!" bubbles Serena. I can't keep my eyes off either one of them—they're both so grown up! Serena observes me in a motherly way and says in what sounds to me like a pseudo-soothing voice, "Hey, Caley, I know what you need—a shower! I'll turn it on for you. You'll feel much better."

"You want me to take my clothes off." *Oh yes, wouldn't that be grand for a camera? If she's going to force me to do that, I'll need to get this man out of my room.* "Ashton—uh, where are you packing to go?"

"Oh, Jesus. Look, Caley, I know I hit you all of a sudden with my wanting to give you that ring. Hell, I'd never even asked you to marry me. But you and I—we never looked at anyone else all through high school and college. Even when I took that year off and went to London *(Oh, now I remember—London, that's where he told me he was going)* after I graduated— I've never said this, Caley—thinking maybe I'd find someone else—crazy, huh? But it was always you. So I just kind of assumed—well, joke's on me."

He sits down on the bed again. "I'll take back the ring. I guess I shouldn't have—look, I don't have to take that job in Boston if you're still so set against it. I mean, if *you'd* gotten a job somewhere and wanted me to pack up and follow you without our talking it over, I'd be mad, too."

"I'm not mad. It's just that—my head hurts a little."

"Get out of that bed and take a shower! Put on some clean clothes! That's the answer! And then I'll help you get packed and you and Ash can get going to Boston! Ooh, I will miss you two so very *very* much!" Serena whisks the pillow away from me and shakes it loose from its case. "Go! I'm stripping this room!" I expect her to start singing "Whistle while you work", she's so damned cheerful. I watch to see if she's playing to one particular part of the room, where the camera would be hidden.

"Wait. I've got another—one question. Where's Doris?"

Relief washes over my friends' faces. "Well, that explains it," says Ashton. "You took something and then must have mixed it with something else at the party. You were so upset that she wasn't going to come to your graduation that you stormed off. You told us you were going to get something to calm yourself down, so you could get through your Class Clown speech."

"Class Clown? I gave a speech?"

"It was hilarious!—don't tell me you don't remember *that*? Well, it will be on somebody's phone. It's on mine." Ashton picks up his cellphone. "Here. Sorry it's from the side. I leaned out as far as I could, to get it. But somebody in the audience will have one with a better view of you."

I stare at the person who doesn't quite look like me. It is indeed a side view and I am looking at a row of gowned men and women, seated. The person the camera is aimed at, wearing a mortarboard and gown, is giving a speech at a podium on a stage; she looks quite animated and self-assured.

"Wow," I say. "Curiouser and curiouser."

"Maybe you took something before you gave your speech, you know, to calm your nerves. And then kept taking stuff at the party on the beach last night. But we both know you don't drink. Who in the world would you trust enough to give you something?"

"Somebody could have slipped her something without her knowing it at the time," says Ashton. His hands are in my hair, on my face, on my arms. He is hugging me to his chest and the warmth, the smell, the very *heartbeat* of him make me dizzy all over again.

"My goodness, Ash, can't you wait until I'm out of the room at least?" Serena says. .I feel like pulling him down on the bed, he looks so genuinely concerned and his touch is causing some feelings I'm unused to stirring inside me, even in the midst of my confusion.

Wait. Don't act all gushy. They're probably filming this.

"All right honey, let's establish that somebody slipped you something, and go from there. Sure, that *must* be it—that would explain everything. Ash. Stop pawing her. Caley. Shower! "

Now I feel my skin in wonder. "It's sandy!" It's also a little rougher than I remember, but I don't say that out loud. Ashton licks my arm. "Also still salty. But I still love you."

"Caley, my goodness. You slept all gritty last night? Give me those sheets."

I will not try to make sense of this. Not right now, I tell myself. Here's the only boy (and now somehow he's a man) I have ever loved and he's licking my arm and he kissed me and he told me that we're engaged and if I've had amnesia from a brain injury and don't remember any of what happened before I woke up, then I'll make the best of it.

Even my hair. "I'll grow it back" I murmur.

"You will? Well, now you're making sense!" Serena exclaims. "And hurry with that shower—I'm getting hunger pangs."

Something pricks at me. "Ashton, can I see your phone again? Where I give my speech?"

He holds it up over my head so I can't reach it and then, laughing, hands it to me. I can't get over what high spirits he is in! And he obviously is crazy about me, that's for certain. Somehow with this amnesia I've missed remembering being courted, have missed remembering the rapture of dating, graduating—*studying!*—have missed tests and final exams and have somehow been able to get through college in this kind of walking waking coma state.

Now I study the cellphone. Ashton has panned around the audience in a rather shaky way and I understand now why: he is laughing at some very witty things I am somehow saying, so that his hand holding the phone trembles slightly as he laughs. And there, there it is: there in the back row, wearing an immense bright purple straw hat as a shade, is a very old woman and she is grinning broadly and applauding.

She is wearing a matching purple dress. With a huge purple bow at the waist. Somehow I am sure that if I were to see her toenails, they would also match.

6

JUNE 2022

The stinging spray of hot water calms me. Obviously I've had some kind of major trauma and I appear to have lost five years of my life.

Five years! I've lost my entire senior year of high school, my high school graduation, four years of college and graduation there too; but along the way I have somehow gone out with Ashton and we've fallen in love and now I'm engaged and about to move to Boston!

I did all that—I somehow passed courses as if I'd been walking in my sleep. So I have no memory of the pain, the sheer drudgery, of studying. Just—*zip!*—and I'm here! Painless, easy even—what was it that high school teacher (Mr. Mariposa, funny how I recall *that*) had said—"Caley, don't choose lazy. Don't take the easy way through life, watching from the sidelines, watching others get involved, so that you're not a participant in your own life"—well, what did *he* know. Here I am, grown up! I lean against the shower wall and laugh in relief.

I run soap over my new body, admiring myself. The soap smells heavenly—must be Serena's choice. And aside from my hair—what was I thinking, doing that? *Yes, what was I thinking all those years that I have no memory of?* It's like I went to bed and woke up five years later.

This reminds me of Dickens' "A Christmas Carol" (how come I can remember *that* and not other more important junk?) and for some reason this settles me—of course! If I have in some mysterious way come to the future, I can maybe just go to sleep and maybe be back in the past again! I'll need to have a consultation with the doctor who cut off my hair and did some kind of brain operation on me.

Unless—unless I'm sleeping and dreaming all this now. But I've never had a dream that was this detailed, this sharp.

Wait. Scrooge had some lesson he needed to learn. And if that's true, then what is mine? I'd better be very, very careful while I figure out what's going on. Crafty. I need to be crafty.

I laugh again: I missed all those years of classes, the grind of studying, taking tests; and overnight I'm a grownup! An engaged, about to be married grownup! To *Ashton*, for god's sake! And I don't know if I had to work to get him or if it just happened! Some fairy godmother has granted me my best wishes and made me, it looks like, quite attractive to boot.

A thought—do I know how to drive? Do I have a driver's license? Have Ashton and I had sex? (This part irrationally annoys me the most—that we may have had sex and I can't remember it.) What do my clothes look like? I must have been buying clothes over these years for this body, without remembering that I was doing so! Oh, this *is* like Christmas, discovering what the grownup me has been doing!

Apparently the grownup me likes Modigliani prints. The kid me never did. *That* I can recall, anyway.

I step out of the shower, walk into the bedroom, a towel wrapped around me just in case their camera is still running—(but, oh, what a movie star body I have!)—and open a closet door.

"Oh, no you don't!" Serena closes it. "As of graduation you're through borrowing my stuff. "

I look around and spot another closet. I open it and gasp: "*All my clothes are purple!*"

"Yeah, no kidding. You told us you were going through a phase and we needed to quit teasing you about it, so you promised that you'd stop wearing this color when you graduated."

"But I don't even *like* purple!"

"Finally—true confessions. Yeah, so it's finally safe to tell you that Ashton and I got pretty tired of it, too. I really tried to get him to stop calling you 'your majesty', but that didn't even get you into something different. Actually, I think that's when the kids started calling you the Class Clown, because of that color. And the hair. For a while until we got really sick of it, you dyed your hair purple, too. So—now you want to take *my* clothes? Uh uh. No way."

But I have gathered up the awful purple-colored shirts and dresses and even jeans—what did I do, *dye* these? I didn't know they made so many outfits in so many shades of this terrible color!—and I have dumped them into a large black garbage bag.

"Done! Now I *have* to wear something of yours." Serena's eyes are wide. "Boy, you really meant it! You sure *are* different today."

"I just decided I like being an adult." I *do*, I realize. "Can we get something to eat? I'm starving."

"Here." Serena tosses me a pair of shorts and a tee shirt. "You don't get my underwear, though. You're going to have to wear your usual until you buy something else." She pulls a drawer from one of the two small dressers in the room—*our college dorm room!* I marvel. *We went to college together!*—and sprinkles underwear onto my bed—all purple.

"Yuck. I can hardly wait to go shopping and replace these things."

"Now that's what I've wanted to hear. I'll be downstairs with Ash. You want to join us when you're ready? Usual place."

"Uh—no." I have no idea what the usual place would be and how to get there. "Wait for me. I'll be just a minute."

As soon as Serena (or her very good impersonator) leaves I talk to the walls: "Okay, the joke's over. I'm in on it, okay? If you want to film me nude, so be it. But don't film this part, because I'm about to steal some of—this other person's underwear!" I rummage through her dresser. I am not about to wear that dreadful eggplanty color next to my skin. Fortunately, her bra fits me adequately enough and so do her panties. I wish I had a full-length mirror to really check out what I look like. If I'm in a female dorm there has to be one close by. I'm itching to get to a store and outfit this new me.

A part of me still wonders what happened to those five years—this has to be some kind of brain injury! When I dropped the wet towel onto the floor nobody popped out of hiding with a camera, nobody burst in screaming with laughter-- so I guess that's not what's going on. What if I just believed them? If I've missed all the tough stuff, well—hooray for me!

I'll need money for new clothes.

In the drawer beside my bed is a purple wallet with a credit card and a driver's license and fifty-three dollars. The photo on the driver's license shows my unsmiling face—it's really me, I really did learn how to drive and I went to the driver's license place and stood in line to have my picture taken, and I don't remember any of this, not at all.

The wallet color and its gaudy sheen hurt my eyes. Someone must have bought me this as a gag gift. I'll need a new one. I study my license: "EXPIRES JANUARY 2024".

I sit down hard on my bed. I never thought about the date changing! Now I feel quite odd and woozy as I contemplate the years I have missed. I think I need someone to examine me and make sure that I haven't been in some kind of fugue state (*Is that the right phrase? How do I know that, unless someone like a doctor has explained it to me?*) or coma. Are there bugs, like the ones that give deer Lyme disease, that could have bitten me and caused this to happen?

Worse, are there places in—2022, it must be now—where they lock up people like me? For the first time I consider the futility of trying to get people to believe me.

Okay, now this is a very chilling idea, being put away for sounding crazy. I'd better keep quiet until I can figure out what I'm doing here and how I got here.

But first I really am starving hungry and I yearn, actually yearn, for Ashton to hold me some more.

7

JUNE 8, 2022 11:15 AM

Nobody stares at us in the (to me, totally unfamiliar) diner. We are just three normal-looking new graduates. The place is crowded with what must also be recent graduates; quite a few of them have stopped at our table to tell me how funny my speech was, not waiting for replies or needing me to call them by name, which is a relief, since none of them look familiar. I listen much more than I talk, although what Serena and Ashton are discussing swirls around me so fast that I feel like a person with bad hearing. I want to cup my hand to an ear the way old people do, to understand all the words.

I smile the way people who can't hear so well smile, too, even at the waitress, who seems to know me and pokes at my arm, her mouth showing a set of chalk-white teeth: "Heard about that wild speech you gave, Caley! Wish I'd been there! We could all use a little more *laughin'* around here nowadays, right?"

She looks pointedly across the room at a couple wearing tee shirts with the words WHITE SUPREMACY and as I follow her gaze I am surprised to see only white people in this diner. She looks at me and nods, not showing any emotion; then shakes herself a little and smiles. "Yep, sure wish I'd been there."

Me too. I hardly notice that she has a little purple handkerchief in her pocket.

Both of my friends react when I say I want new clothes. "There's a terrific consignment shop downtown," says Serena. I'm afraid to ask where downtown is. Banana Bay never has never had an uptown or a downtown, either. But we must be in Banana Bay, because my diploma had read "Banana Bay College", although there never has been a college here that I can recall.

I have never been in this diner, either.

"No," I answer firmly, so no one will know how shaky I feel. "I want all new clothes." *For my new body*, I think. Then I remember the bathing suit I'd tried on yesterday. "Macy's! Let's go there!"

"Caley, that place closed last year when buying went bigtime online and everyone started using drones."

"Oh yeah, sure. I forgot. I meant to say, 'A place like Macy's,' "

"Well—we'd have to go to Orlando, with not much to pick from— I mean in person—here in Banana Bay. But look, just go to one of the websites and you can have whatever you want in hours. I'll lend you a few things in the meantime. Gives me a chance to refresh, too."

"Women and shopping." Ashton gets up. "I'll take care of the check. I have to be out of the fraternity house by noon and I still can't find a pair of my favorite jeans." He stretches and yawns. *His body is like a well-trained athlete's! And he's chosen me!* He closes his mouth and smiles down at me. His eyes are sky-blue and the thought of being with him for the rest of my life almost makes me shake with desire. And I haven't done a thing I remember to earn it!

"Hey, Serena. I don't see your old boyfriend around here, after you broke his heart."

"Yes, well, you know I've only been in love with you, Ash." We all laugh, their laughter loud, mine polite.

Is she kidding? I can't be sure. *Well, he's mine, not hers*, I think smugly. "Serena," I interrupt, "what does your religion call it when you get something that you don't deserve and that you haven't earned?"

"Well, aren't you something, to remember that?" marvels Serena. "Grace. It's called grace, just like our waitress's name over there."

"Huh. Odd."

"But Ashton, if you're planning on leaving this afternoon, how are we supposed to have enough time to get to Orlando and back?"

"Caley, look—just spend an hour at that store Serena told you about. Get what you need there, just some basics, and we'll fix you up better when we get to Boston. Just, I beg of you, nothing in that color-that-we-don't-ever-discuss."

"But—we haven't even talked about when and where we're getting married."

Again there is an odd look that passes between Ashton and Serena. "Honey, look at the ring finger on your right hand," Serena points.

I look. There is a little orange mark where, if I wore a ring on that hand, the jewel would be. Ashton holds out his right hand. He has an identical mark. "We were married yesterday afternoon."

"We're—married!" I try to sound more excited than shocked.

"It was *your* idea, Caley. *I* was against it." Serena bounces a little in her seat.

"Yeah, Serena here, such a wedding planner, wanted to make it a big fancy affair. But you said, 'Why wait—we'll have to show proof when we leave Florida, anyway.' And it's not as though we could have a big church wedding, since you've never gone to church and most of them have been shut down, anyway." Serena frowns at this.

What has happened in the past five years? It's as though there has been some kind of reorganization that I've missed. "So this finger—"

"Oh, look at her!" Serena snorts. "Bad enough that the churches have been closed. Doesn't matter to you, of course. But I always dreamed of being married in the place where I went every Sunday. It was like my second home." She and Ashton exchange a look. "Given Caley's sudden recent loopiness, it's a good thing you haven't told her—"

"Not here," Ashton cautions her as he looks around the diner.

So we're married, I think. *And I guess I just stick my finger out and something reads whatever I have had inserted in there and it tells whoever needs to know, that I'm half of a couple. And Ashton has the same thing. We have no wedding rings. Guess we don't need them.*

But what if people divorce? is my next thought, a wildly zany one. *Does the finger have to be removed? Is that how the government knows if you're married or not?*

"Pretty crappy, huh?"

Startled by the word, I look up at him. He is grinning. He turns to the other people in the diner. "Hey, Caley and I got married yesterday. Crappy!"

And now the dozen people still here and the waitress named Grace are yelling, "Crappy!" and applauding. I hold up my right hand and wiggle the fourth finger. "Crappy!" I cry.

8

Ashton and Serena are leaving, in opposite directions—Ashton to pack and Serena to pick up something she left at her former boyfriend's apartment. I breathe a sigh of relief. We have coordinated our times on some generic-looking identical watches (Before we left the diner Ashton proudly presented me with mine, wrapped in some newspaper—"no time to get anything fancier," he grinned), and he has warned me to be back at my dorm by two o'clock.

Now here's a problem, if we all go in separate directions: when Serena and I walked to this diner I wasn't paying attention, so I have no idea how to get back to the dorm.

Crafty. Be crafty. "Hey, guys!" I tell them brightly, "I just want to walk around a little, say good-by to my Florida past before we head out. How about we just meet back here at the diner?"

"Fine with me," says Ashton distractedly; and then to my surprise he kisses me, hard, while Serena looks away. "More later," he whispers. I nod. He waves as he lopes down the street.

"But you haven't packed yet!" protests Serena, frowning. "And you know the law. It's not really safe to be a female alone, even in the daytime." But I'm not listening to her. I'm distracted by the thought: *Oh boy. I wonder if she keeps track of her underwear; she's going to be missing a pair. I may get in trouble with her over this.*

But she really is my old friend. "Look, Caley, you don't have any clothes to fold, thank God. Let's forget the shopping. I'll box up the items you have—and this way I'll know if you're making off with any of mine!" (*If she only knew.*) "It's the least I can do for you. Okay, I'll bring it all back here and I'll get to say good-by to you again." Her eyes fill up with tears. "Oh, I'm going to miss you and Ash! This will be the first time you and I have been apart!"

"How about-- when I was in the *hospital*?" I ask in what I think is a very cunning way, trying to see if there's any information I can get from her without having to sound as though I don't know what I'm talking about.

"The hospital?"

"Yeah, you know. That time--."

"Oh, Caley. *That* doesn't count. For heaven's sake, a little strep throat and you think you're on death's door. And I *was* there at the hospital, you ninny--."

"Right. Just checking. Hey--thanks for packing for me. I'll see you here at two."

"Don't forget to say good-by to the plaque of Ben and Anna Bayh for good luck. And please be careful!" and she is gone, running up the street faster than I have ever seen her move. That weight-loss program seems like a miracle.

But if I haven't been in the hospital, that must rule out brain surgery, right?

I head for a little park across the street from the diner. As long as I can see the place from here, I'll be safe. I'll just wait for them here. I wish idly that I had something to read. At the entrance is a wooden board showing a carving of two people dressed in old-fashioned costumes, the wood a weathered gray—must be old Ben and Anna—with some historical data, it looks like, of Banana Bay.

I'm distracted from reading it, because what has caught my eye is the statue of a man on a horse, in the center of the park near a grandstand. The statue appears to be so new that it almost looks wet. When the sun hits it there is a reflection which hurts my eyes.

I move close to it and stare at the man. He is in garishly-colored military dress; his red hair, which has to be a dye job for a man his age, is in a short modern cut, his hands beefy and outspread, so that he looks as though without holding onto the reins he is daring the horse to bolt. A large shiny plaque reads THE ROYAL PLEASANTNESS 2018-, but he doesn't look royal or pleasant—instead he looks overweight, self-satisfied and rather repellent, his mouth set in a firm line and his eyes hard.

He looks familiar and yet I can't recall ever having seen him, so I wander away from the statue to a shadier spot, where I sit down on one of two wooden benches, both painted a fading green.

I wish I'd asked at the diner for a bottle of water. The Florida sun beats down on me. But just look at how my diamond sparkles in the sunlight! I am fascinated by the rainbow colors it reflects onto my leg: red, orange, yellow, green, blue, indigo—indigo—whatever has happened to violet? How odd.

"Nah. What's violet, except a nice fancy-schmancy way of sayin' 'purple'?"

I look up, shading my eyes against the glare. I wonder idly if I'll need to buy sunglasses for Boston. "Excuse me?"

"Hey, Caley. How ya doin'? Takin' the easy route through life? Enjoyin' yourself?"

This person knows my name. Then I take another look—oh, no wonder. It's our waitress from the diner. "I'm sorry. Do I know you, other than as our—other than in the diner?" What had Serena called her? Oh, yes. "Grace, right?"

"*Amazin'* Grace," the waitress says, and plops herself supine on the grass a few feet away from me. "Except that's not my real name. Pseudonym, you'd call it. Soodo-*nim*. I'm still waitin' for my real one, so I'm tryin' out others in the meantime. Did you know it's illegal for a robot to choose a name for itself? Now that's just downright insensitive. Boy, that waitressin' work is hard on the dogs." She hands me a bottle of cold water.

"The—the dogs?"

"The tootsies, the dogs, the feet. I wasn't countin' on fallen arches."
She chortles: "Fallen *arches*, not fallen *angels*—that's a good one! I'll have
to remember that one. Won't be hard, 'cause next to you, my memory is
totally untarnished."

"Uh huh." Whoa--this woman may be mental. I stand up and smile
politely. "Well, nice chatting with you. Thanks for the water. (*I'll examine
it later, to make sure it hasn't been tampered with.*) I need to be going now—"

"Don't you care to know where you've been these past five years, between Macy's and this warm kind of reunion? And I told you my name
isn't actually Grace. That's just kind of an inside joke for me. But I *do* think
of myself as amazing. Did you notice how my voice changed just now from
hard-boiled waitress to old softy me? I told you I do voices." She sounds
quite proud of herself.

I find that I've sat down again. "Whoops, got yourself a weak-knees
moment there, Caley?"

"What--what are you talking about?"

"I'm talking about how you can't remember the past five years, and
good ones they were, too. But you were in a hurry to grow up. So, ta-dah,
here you are, talking to a waitress, an eyeblink later."

"Who are you?"

"Jes' a little ole server from ole Banana Bay--"

"Who *are* you?"

"*WHO IS THIS THAT DARKENS COUNSEL BY WORDS
WITHOUT KNOWLEDGE? WHERE WERE YOU WHEN I LAID
THE FOUNDATION OF THE EARTH?*" Her voice is deep and com-
manding and I fall to my trembling knees without thought.

"What--?"

"Check that bench you just fell off of, "she says in a normal tone.

"Wait! What was that you just said?"

"Scare you a little?" I nod. "Good. That's my God imitation. Nothing
like God's, actually—but *you* wouldn't know for sure anyway, now would
you, since you haven't tried to listen?"

"I don't have any idea what you're talking about!"

"Okey-dokey. Back to the benchmark. Go ahead. Run your fingers over it, just three inches this side of your left hand. See what I mean?"

I feel carved indented markings in the soft wood before I actually see the words "ASH LOVES CALEY 2020." There's a little logo of eyeglasses beside my name. It is obvious that the markings are not fresh.

"Twenty-twenty, that was the year, the year you and Ash got really serious about each other. Oh sure, there were a couple other girlfriends for him, *lots* of other boyfriends for you, including the one that you took away from Serena—I always felt particularly sorry for Owen—she was crazy about him and they would have made a positive match, would have changed the future of the planet in their own way, for the good". . . . She studies me. "Boy, you and Ashton—all the shouting, misunderstandings, reconciliations, before you got to this point on this bench. Ashton's got himself a heap of patience and quite a sense of humor, so he added the glasses—twenty-twenty, get it?"

I am baffled. "I don't get-- *anything.*"

"You almost remembered it all, studying that statue. But it was just a *little* too much hard work for you, wasn't it? Hey, here's a riddle for you: 'What do you call it when a fake horse has to carry a fake horse's ass? The Royal Turd.' Good, huh? I would have liked credit for it, but that's what people all around the U.S. of A. are saying about that guy over there. Some factory's been ordered to turn them out like hotcakes for all the parks, national, state, and as you see here—local. They're painted acrylic of some kind, like surfboards."

"Make sense, will you please, Grace?"

"Told you—that's not my name. You're going through life the easy way, kid. You got your wish. Well, not truly a wish—wishes don't come with strings attached."

"So—do you know *this* about me: that I *don't* have any brain damage. No walking and waking coma, no fugue state?"

"Nada. Just me. Me and your need to grow up, my cute little anti-Peter Pan."

The way she talks in ellipses I am finding infuriating—not to mention that I am in a conversation with a voice-changing waitress! "So—tell me. What do I *do?*"

"The wheels are already in motion, kid. Next time you see me you're going to be six years older, without having to lift a finger." She hoists herself off the grass and brushes her uniform with both hands. "Gotta get back to work. Those plates don't serve themselves."

"Wait! Don't go!"

She laughs as though she knows a private joke. "Those may become our favorite conversations together: 'Stop! Wait! Don't go!', but life doesn't work that way. And it doesn't *ever* go backward. I already told you that."

"When the hell did you tell me that?"

"Dressing room. Bikini bathing suit. Hah?" I strain my brain to remember. Wisps of memory float through my head, too distant from my consciousness for me to be able to study them.

"Wait!" I call her. She is skipping across the lawn to the street. Now I notice that she is wearing some very sturdy-looking purple sneakers. "Whatever this is, I didn't ask for it!" I yell.

"You didn't ask to be born, either; but here you are."

"You need to *explain* to me! Wait! Wait!"

"We're *wait-ing*!" And there are Serena and Ashton in what looks like a brand-new car, Serena singing and waving to me. I don't recognize the make of the car, not that it matters, except that I need *something* right now to be familiar and recognizable—a VW, a Ford truck. The waitress with the purple shoes is nowhere to be seen.

"Where did she go?"

"Who go?"

"That waitress—the one you called Grace." They both look at me in puzzlement and a look passes between them.

"Been sleeping?" Serena and Ashton sit down, one on either side of me. "Wow. You must have been sleeping hard—you have marks on your face from pressing into the bench."

"It's a wonder you weren't picked up by a robot. If they scanned you out here they could have traced you to me, and there would go my job. You can't just go to sleep on a park bench, like a vagrant," mutters Ashton.

"But look, Ash—it makes a nice omen." Serena points to my face and pulls out a little cosmetic mirror. "Here, Caley." And there on my cheek is the impression "2020" and the glasses.

The 2020 is the wrong way, of course, spelling out 0202; but the eye-glasses look correct enough, forward or backward.

9

JUNE 2022

Ashton and I are sitting in his brand-new car, according to him a perk given by the Massachusetts company he will be working for. The car is heading north. The car is driving itself! We have just made love in his car in broad daylight, in the seats which fold back and become a camping bed or sleeping place for the kiddies, depending on one's lifestyle. Or a marriage bed.

We just made love at one hundred ten miles per hour while technology hurtles us up I-95 in line with the other self-driving cars. Since there are apparently not many of these on the market yet, we have a lane mostly to ourselves, to keep us from the actual "old-fashioned" drivers who might endanger us.

When I say "old-fashioned", Ashton laughs in a harsh rueful way. "You still can't call them 'Recyclables' the way The Royal Pleasantness wants, can you? Good for you. And you're so funny about not liking to swear. Your mother can swear like a Marine."

Doris. "Where is she? How is she?" I pull away from Ashton so that I can study his face.

"Who knows? No word, no call, no, 'Go to hell' for The Royal you-know-who, even. I hated to see you so broken up about her not being there yesterday for your graduation."

"Forget it. I—I've forgotten it already." He can't know how true that is.

The car's robotic voice suddenly announces, "Border in twenty minutes. First warning."

"Uh oh," Ashton grabs for his shirt. "We need to get dressed. Now look, Caley, I've been through this before. Don't talk. I'll do all the talking. No jokes, no games. They *will* shoot. Here's a disinfecting wipe—get all the smell of me off your right hand and especially your ring finger."

"But—"

"Just be thorough. If they can't read your marker they won't ask questions. I'm telling you they will shoot. And they don't miss. They don't do emotions, so everything is serious business." He is rubbing at his right hand and his ring finger, so I follow his lead.

At the entrance to Georgia to my surprise I catch a glimpse of barbed wire and stacked rifles. The place is so brightly lit that there are no shadows on the concrete, even though it's afternoon. Facing us is a bus, apparently entering Florida. The people filling the vehicle all have white or gray hair or are bald. I catch the glint from many pairs of glasses. No one is smiling.

A woman in a military uniform shines a strong light into the car, although I almost laugh at how unnecessary it seems. Ashton scowls at me.

"How many?" I hear the trunk lid pop open and then slam shut, followed by the engine lid's going up, which gives us a momentary bit of shade. Someone bangs on the top of our car ("Looking for a false roof," Ashton whispers.)

"I repeat. How many?"

"Two. Just married."

"Married?"

"Yes."

"Proof."

Ashton holds out his right hand and she passes a detector over it. It beeps. "Reason for emigrating?"

"I have a new job in Massachusetts."

"Proof." To my surprise he holds out his right wrist and the detector passes over it. It beeps. "Next person."

"That's me," I say.

The officer says sternly, "You do not talk unless I talk to you." I erase my smile. "Proof."

I hesitate.

"*Proof!*"

Ashton, his face pale, grabs my right hand and holds it up for the officer, gripping my wrist so tightly I think I will cry out. The detector beeps.

"Uh--what would happen if I didn't have a right hand?" I ask, to break the tension. The officer starts at this and suddenly beams the light full in my face. Ashton tightens his grip.

"A joke?"

"No, Commander, it is not," he answers before I can say anything.

The light is switched off. "Go and do not stop."

"Yes. I know the rules." He gives the robot driver some commands and the car starts up. The lights fade behind us. I rub my wrist. "What the hell--?" I start.

"What the hell were you trying to do?" Ashton says at the same time.

"What *was* that, anyway?"

"Caley, you act as if you haven't watched tv in years—"

"—or read a paper," I say. *Wait, that's an idea. I'll catch up that way.*

He stares at me. "There aren't any papers anymore. Are you kidding me?" He frowns. "Look, whatever somebody fed you or gave you to drink when we were all on the beach—that should have worn off by now. When we get to Boston we're going to get you looked at. Should've done that before we left Banana Bay."

Now *I'm* scared. "Ashton, are you—regretting being with me?"

"I love you, Caley. Sorry I was so nervous back there. We just have the other state checkpoints to go through --Connecticut's will be easy; they have more cheerful Commanders-- and then we're almost to *Boston*! Oh, Caley, you're going to love it there! The place is full of patriots like us! " He raises his voice in his excitement.

"Patriots. The New England Patriots have won—"

"Cancel!" Ashton tells the robot.

"Understood."

"Whisper," he tells me.

"Okay," I whisper back. But what's the big deal about getting out of Florida?"

"Hey, I know how much you hate politics, but you act as though you've had your head under a rock," he says, and grabs at my short hair playfully. "Huh—maybe you hit your head on something—a coquina rock, maybe."

"Maybe."

"Well, that would explain your short-term memory loss. Okay, we have one more Georgia checkpoint then one more Carolina—"

"Two. North and South Carolina. I know *that* much."

"Ha ha yourself—they merged six months ago. With Virginia. Forget?"

"Just testing you," I say weakly. I feel as though my head is going to spin off. So many changes!

"Next border in thirty minutes," says the robotic voice.

"Has that guy been listening to us?" I know I had made sounds during sex and my face flushes, even though it may have just been a mechanical device within earshot.

"This one will be easier. That last one, they just wanted to check that we weren't smuggling anyone old out of Florida. They *will* check the car again, though, so don't say anything suspicious. I know some guys who smart-mouthed a Commander at the northern Georgia border, and they were dragged out of their car and beat up. Damned Florida, bowing to the President and caving in to all his orders the way they did. And one wise-ass south Florida senator convincing him we could build a canal from east to west at the northern border—and fill it with gators—what a damned stupid thing to propose! And the President crazy enough to think that was a crappy idea. You remember *that*, don't you?"

"Oh—oh sure, I remember *that*," I answer. "Boy, that was—a not-crappy idea, all right!"

"If the President couldn't build a wall someplace, he was determined to dig that canal—they argued about it in Congress for nine months after his inauguration, until a couple of Senators got shot and killed, one right out in the open and the other inside the Senate chamber by the President's KKK military, and that shut everyone up. Stupid thing to argue about, a canal, when the state's already become the first Recycling Center. Well, that's what comes of having a narcissistic President and an equally un-hinged Governor and a bunch of cowards in Congress. It was a perfect storm of toadies and gun-toting psychotics. *Everyone* just caved, especially when the Supreme Court was declared un-American. You know all this, though. I'm sorry to give a lecture. It just makes me so damned mad."

"Are—we safe enough in here talking about this then?" *I can't believe it! Senators were killed and the government has changed so radically so fast! Why didn't I pay more attention in Mr. Mariposa's class?* For the first time I feel the weight of having wasted time as such a smart-ass in school.

"Caley, I'll tell you what it felt like to me: like a Florida sinkhole, where you have no idea that there's anything going on right underneath your feet; and all the time the limestone underground is eroding away until all of a sudden your car and house are in a hole thirty feet across and just as deep. *And* just as sudden—wham! Just like that!"

"There are no known sinkholes this far north of the Florida state line—"

"Cancel," Ashton says.

"Understood."

I shudder. I've seen pictures of sinkholes and they are deadly and, as Ashton says, without warning. "Are we safe?" I repeat. "I mean about—him. Uh—it."

"Yeah, we're safe enough. This guy's been programmed to respond only to words about the trip. Wisdom!" he yells, startling me. There is no response from the car. "Donut!"

"There is a donut shop in seven miles."

"See?" Ashton tells me. To the robot he says, "Cancel donuts."

"Understood."

"Aw—I could have used a donut," I say. Ashton's face is so serious that I want to jolly him out of his mood.

"There is a donut shop in six miles."

"Cancel," Ashton says.

"Understood."

"Hey," I whisper, "we didn't say anything car-like while we were hav-ing sex, did we?"

"Just once—I cancelled it before you knew what was happening." He pulls out a laptop computer with an unusual metallic lid. "Mind if I do some research about my new job?"

"No. It's okay." I need time to think. Somehow life has altered furiously in the past five years and I have daydreamed through it all. I'll need a crash course to figure it out.

"Ashton, I need to take a—" I stop myself. I almost said "crash" and who knows how the robot would react to that? Ashton doesn't look up from the laptop. There are symbols on its screen that I never seen before. I'll need a course in that, too, I guess. Unless it's like the driver's license and I learned it without remembering that I did. I hope that's the case—it looks difficult to figure out. "A nap. I need to take a nap."

"There are extra pillows and blankets beneath the back deck. You should not need the blankets, since the month is June and the temperature outside is eighty-nine degrees. Inside the vehicle it is seventy-two degrees. It is sixty-seven degrees at our destination Boston at the current moment. . . "

"Cancel," I say.

"Proof."

"What?"

"Proof."

"Cancel," says Ashton.

"Understood."

"Caley, I need to get your voice recognized by this thing after we get to Boston."

"Boston was founded in the year. . . "

"Cancel."

"Understood."

He looks at me, a little sheepish. "Few bugs still in the system," he whispers. He returns to his laptop. "Okay?"

I nod. And I, I am the "take the easy path" person who knows and cares so little about political government, who gets bored with the articles in the newspaper and would much rather read the horoscope page and the movie reviews (I guess now it's too late for that, with no newspapers— how could they shut all *those* down?), am too reluctant to press him for more information. All that in a couple of days or years, whether I believe my own sense of time or that of the weird waitress. What the hell had I taken, to do this to me? Brain damage, some tremendous kind of trauma, something like that. I think I must be doing a great job of convincing Ashton I know all that's going on, when actually I am scared all the way down to my purple sneakers.

("Honey, you have to have something on your feet for up north. My shoes wouldn't fit you, or I'd give you a pair of those," Serena had told me, handing me a small suitcase, which demonstrated to me that without purple clothing, I really didn't have much to my name.)

My name! Which is now Mrs. Ashton Reed! Funny how those sneakers are the same color as the waitress'—maybe there was a sale somewhere. I sure hope there are good stores in Boston for shopping.

I take comfort in telling myself that whatever this is will wear off and I am apparently very safe with Ashton, as long as I follow his lead and don't try to act as though I know more than I do.

And so we stay awake until we have passed through the second check-point and Ashton has breathed a deep sigh of relief. When in Delaware I say I'd like to stop for coffee, Ashton tells me (and so does the robotic voice), "Coffee will be ready in thirty seconds—cream or sugar, please?"; but when I say I also need a bathroom break, I am interested to see that no car manufacturer has figured out yet how to do that (for a female, anyway); and the robotic voice is silent.

There are no more problems at the state guard stations. The rest area that the car finds for us is clean and quiet. And despite the caffeine, I am so exhausted from all that has gone on this day that I curl up beside Ashton and the green glow of his laptop. The last thing I hear before falling into a deep dreamless sleep is his voice whispering comfortingly into my ear, "Next stop—Connecticut, then our new home!"

10

OCTOBER 2028
BOSTON

I wake up in a huge bed in an unfamiliar room, to the sound of rain. *I must be upstairs*, I think, hearing the murmur of distant voices coming from below. *How nice of Ashton to have carried me up here. Oh Ashton, Ashton*—shades of Scarlett O'Hara. I grin at the idea of me in a hoop skirt, Ashton in knee-high riding boots. Oh, I do love the sound of a man in creaking leather. . .

The smell of toast and coffee wafts in under the doorsill and brings me to wide-awake now, and I slide out of bed and go to the window. I am wearing what looks like a very expensive nightgown and I blush with smugness at the idea of my new husband's undressing me last night.

I must have been sound asleep not to remember that. And he's quite tidy—there's not a sign of my discarded clothing in sight. I have married a treasure. I'll have to take a page from his book and learn to be less messy.

Outside, the rain and the clouds have given the street and the buildings a gray cast and I am delighted to see that we are in a brownstone amidst a row of brownstone houses—at least the ones on the other side of the street are. Edwardian? Victorian? It doesn't matter: I've never lived in anything so grand. There are only a few leaves on the trees that line the street, I note. That's strange for June. Maybe things flower in different seasons up here.

The ceiling in this bedroom is a high one and quite ornate. I spot a bit of water stain in one corner, but these old houses must certainly need care, that's for sure. There is a chandelier hanging from the center of the figured ceiling. Together they look like the icing on a fancy wedding cake. I look around for the wall switch, to play with it and admire the lights both on and off in each shiny upturned glass chandelier cup. It also boasts—I think that is the word-- crystal pendants which catch the light and I am almost hypnotized, standing beneath them.

How beautiful this will be on a sunshiny day with rainbows dancing around the walls!

Back at the window I can see there's a park in the middle of the divided street and it contains a statue—to my wonderment, it's a replica of a man on a horse, the very same one I saw yesterday in Banana Bay. Someone with a bright purple umbrella is the only one I can spot up or down this boulevard, and this person—can't tell by the way the umbrella is held, whether it's a man or a woman--is in the park area, holding a leash. At the other end tugs a damp cheerful-looking Scotty. I think it's a Scotty—at any rate, it's a small dog, its belly low to the wet grass.

All of a sudden the umbrella is snapped shut. It's a man, I can see now, in a tropics-printed purple poncho. *Plastic purple poncho*, I think, and this wordplay makes me laugh. The man looks up, as though he has heard me. He waves to me and I wave back. I can swear the dog is waving a paw, too.

I am so excited to learn about my new house and neighborhood—I'll look for an umbrella myself and go adventuring. I've never lived anywhere except Florida, have never seen snow, have never known a gray drizzly day like this. It is all so novel that I feel like a child exploring a Disney king-dom without the crowds. My heart will explode, I'm sure of it, with the idea of Ashton to love and have love me the way we went at it yesterday, and this wonderful new world!

The bathroom is huge—bigger than two bedrooms combined in my mother's and my apartment I lived in (*how long ago? Hard to recall now*)-- and marbled, with a porcelain tub big enough for two people, I think in de-light, remembering Ashton all over again from the day before in the car.

The toilet is so old-fashioned that it has a tank over it and a pullchain for flushing.

I wash my hands and face, lowering my head over the heavy square white sink. The welcome hot water rises steaming and occludes the mirror above. Without wanting to examine my Florida-tanned complexion yet, or fix my hair, I retreat to luxuriate in bed. I'm still tired, a little stiff from the ride, and not ready yet for breakfast or for moving day, although Ashton had told me this place we were moving into is furnished. I'll sleep another hour and then get up and examine our new home.

"You're up! You're finally, finally up!" A woman enters the bedroom without knocking and falls onto my bed. "Oh, I know, it's miserable weather out there, but it's so cozy downstairs—there's a fire in the fireplace, even-- and I've been waiting just *hours* for you to wake up!"

Well yes, I am now wide awake. Is this kind of familiar bed-sharing the way they do things up north? "Excuse me," I say, and the woman turns over and grins warmly.

My god. It is Serena. How did she get here so fast? I didn't know she was coming. Her hair is a different color and she is wearing glasses, of all things. "What--?"

"You've *got* to get up. The boys insisted on making breakfast for me and now they're waiting for you. They wanted to bring you a tray, but I don't trust them on those stairs with heavy things and they wouldn't let me carry one myself, so there you are. They said they'll serve you in the den, in front of the fire. Doesn't that sound sweet? *I've* already thanked them for my burnt toast and canned applesauce. Ashton wouldn't let them make coffee, of course, and I can't figure out your new gadget, so you *have* to come downstairs and show me how to work it. Oh, and the boys have invented some kind of story that they want to act out, and they're dying to show it to us. That one they did last night before bed was just priceless. Oh, Caley, you are so lucky!"

I can't believe we have servants and that Serena, this different-appearing Serena, is so --on such close terms with them. Things really are different up here. Why would we want the hired help to put on a show for us?

She watches me. "What is it? Here. Take your bathrobe. I must say you don't seem very enthusiastic. I know you don't like to share them with me, but how often do I see them?"

"What? How --how did you get here so fast?"

"Fast? That plane must have stopped at every airport. I swear, the number of times we were processed—well, we were all just automatically sticking out our hands after a while, for a Commander. We had to wash every time we accidentally touched another person. I tell you, it's pretty dangerous to be nice to anyone anymore."

"What are you talking about? Who are the boys? How many servants do we have?"

"You don't have servants, you ninny. I'm talking about the children."

"But—where did you get the children?"

"Got them from their beds—what did you think--that they're *mine?* Not that I wouldn't love to take them back to Florida with me. If I could get them away from Ashton, of course. And the border patrol—boy, they'd be checking my pelvis for illegal activity--. Sorry. I shouldn't have joked like that. Even up here the walls might have ears." Again she stops and looks at me. "Damned shame that children aren't allowed in Florida anymore."

"I'm—feeling a little dizzy."

"I told you last night that wine and rum don't mix. But no, have you ever listened to me?"

I can hear shouts and laughter from somewhere outside my bed-room—would it be downstairs?

"They want you up, Caley. 'Get Mom!' they kept yelling, even though *I* kept telling them that you needed to sleep. I cannot imagine the kind of hangover you must have after last night. When did you learn to drink alcohol? Oh, I had to keep hushing them and I read them stories to keep them from pounding on your door—"

"Get Mom. They said, 'Get Mom'? " *I have boys. I have two sons. Any daughters? How did that happen? Did I have a kind of waking coma again?* "Serena, what's the date?"

"If I tell you, will you get up then?" she says teasingly. I nod. "Well, it's the year of The Royal Pleasantness 2028. October nineteenth, to be exact.

Ten forty-seven a.m., to be even more exact. So you can see why they want you to eat breakfast. It's more like brunch by now."

2028. Last night it was 2022. I have lost six more years overnight.

Alarmed, I run into the bathroom and look into the mirror. My face is rounder and I have gray in my curly brown hair. I must have had it, for some incredible reason, dyed and permed—I've always been a blonde. I've always liked being a blonde. I sit at the edge of the tub, trying to remember. I rub my abdomen and discover a little unwelcome softness there instead of the firm stomach I had yesterday. I wonder irrationally if those sons are twins.

Serena is busy making the bed—"so you won't be tempted to get back in it," she sings. "Come on—I need coffee."

"Where's Ashton?"

"What do you do, go to sleep at night and forget everything about your life?" she says lightly.

"Yes."

"What do you mean, yes?" Serena now eyes me suspiciously. "Caley. What are your sons' names?"

"I don't know."

"How about their ages?"

"I don't know. I don't know!" I look at my old friend in desperation.

"Is this—is this like last time? When you didn't know you'd been married?"

"How did you know that I didn't remember that?"

"You were wearing the same expression you have now. Jesus, Caley--!"

"I know. Somehow I've lost the last six years of my life."

"But nobody *does* that!" She hugs me hard. "Look, you need to get up, get dressed, see the boys—something will trigger your memory. It has to!"

"Serena—what are their names?"

"Way—no, I'm not going to tell you. You go downstairs, look them in the eye, give them a hug—for god's sake, just hug them kiss them, *smell* them! You'll remember!"

Way—one of them is Way-- something. "Waylon. Wayfarer. Wayfaring stranger. Way—Wait a minute! Uh—Waiter! And I just yell, 'Waiter!'

when I want him," I search my friend's face for a smile. There is none, not a trace. Underneath my kidding I am terrified.

"Not funny. Here." Serena has found me some jeans and a flannel shirt and I dress fast. They fit, so they must be mine. Serena knew where to find them, so maybe she's the one who put the nightgown on me last night. . .

"Your hair's a mess. Never mind. And why you *ever* did what you did to Ashton I will *never* understand, but he's forgiven you, so I guess I have to, too."

"Uh—I thought your God told you that you *have* to forgive," I murmur, wildly wondering what I could have done to hurt my husband. Serena scowls. "You're right, although it sure was *hard,* you foolish, foolish idiot. At least the boys didn't find out. Now. Just come on. And not that you might care, but Ash was very lucky to get the last flight into Boston from London. The Royal Pleasantness has finally done what he threatened for years—he's shut down all international travel. That will make things tougher for the Global Resis--. Never mind. You're not listening."

"H-m-m?" I'm examining the clothing labels while Serena waits by the door, her arms crossed in impatience, for any kind of clue, but all I can discover is that I am a size ten now, instead of my teenaged six.

Outside the bedroom and down a short hallway is a set of carpeted stairs in a straight run. The carved wooden bannister feels cool and smooth to my touch, and when I raise my hand, it brings with it a faint scent of lemon polish. There is no sound now from the first floor. I can see an antique stained glass door ahead as I descend. I stop at the bottom of the stairs and look around, baffled. There's an enticing odor of burning wood coming somewhere to my left. None of this is familiar. But why should it be? We arrived here last night in the dark and I was asleep.

A wave of paranoia washes over me: Ashton and Serena are still making up some cruel joke, playing it on me, but it's not going to work. I don't know what their motivation is, but I've never had children and only last night Ashton and I were in the car, coming from Florida.

Or maybe the night before—I may have slept an entire day and night. I really was exhausted—I remember that. So if I can remember *that,* then I surely would remember being pregnant—

Serena has moved around me and through a door to my right. Now I can smell the burnt toast. This in itself is sickening, bringing back the meager days in the apartments with Doris.

"They're gone."

"Sure they are. Ha ha."

"No, the car's gone from the portico too, and so is Ashton. He said he was going to take them to the Hall of The Royal Pleasantness, but I guess I told him I wasn't that interested in recent history—'The paint's not even dry in that place,' I told him, but it's in the former Symphony Hall and you know him and his interest in anything Boston, old or new. He told me about how furious he was when the KKK Army set fire to the warship "Constitution" and tore down Bunker Hill; but he said at least he'd already taken the boys to those and he even secretly took pictures. My God, Caley, he could have been arrested, and then what would have happened to the boys? They would have just been left there on the street by themselves! Sometimes he just--!"

"Stop, Serena. Stop. Please. You're saying all these things to confuse me." A thought is weighing me down—that I have two sons. Apparently I have been in this house long enough to get pregnant, go through child-birth and raise infants, then toddlers, then children and I don't know their names or their ages and if I were in the midst of a crowd of children, would not be able to pick out my own. Through some demented twist of fate I have missed out on all of the most significant parts of my life.

I don't even know if I've been tested for any brain disease or not. I just know that at this moment I need Ashton to be here and tell me what a fine time they've been having at my expense. But why? What do they get from it? I've seen the film "Gaslight". Is that what this is?

"Serena. Do you want Ashton and my sons for yourself?"

My friend stares at me. "Is that it? You want Ashton? I know how buddy-buddy you two have been for"-- *for how long?* I have no idea.

"All right. You are now officially crazy." She looks at my troubled face and impulsively hugs me. "I didn't mean that, Caley. It's just that you're being so. . . "

The smell of her Chanel is overpowering, and now it clings to me. "Serena, excuse me, but I need to lie down."

"Wow—you're pasty. Oh Lord, you're not pregnant! You know the law!"

This is an entirely new idea. What law would tell me how many children to have? I shake my head to assuage her. "Please, I have to—"

"Okay, but show me how to turn on that coffee thingy first. "

"I—can't right now. I'm sorry."

"Oh, hell. All right, I'll have to do it the old-fashioned way." She takes a cellphone from her pocket. I am relieved—we still have cellphones! "I want to order two large coffees—"

"Decaf," I mutter.

"They only have regular anymore, since The Royal Pleasantness government took over the franchises. If you want decaf you'll have to make it yourself."

She speaks into the cellphone. "Yes, that's correct." She puts the cellphone back into her pocket. "They've already traced me to this address. It's '1984' all over again. . . "

There is the sound of a bell at the front door. "Fast, huh? Why am I not surprised? Sometimes they're listening to every word and sometimes they don't bother."

I head up the stairs. "Hey, Caley, where are you--?"

"I just have to lie down and close my eyes. I'm really feeling dizzy. I think I may throw up."

The bell sounds again. Serena looks at me, alarmed. As I plod heavily past her, stumbling toward the stairway, she seems to blur.

"Okay, okay—I'll bring your breakfast up to you. Oh Caley, please don't be pregnant." I hear her open the front door, but I have dragged myself up the stairs hand over hand, as if I weigh hundreds of pounds. It's a pressure I recall, that of feeling as though I'm on a planet with a huge gravity, pulling me toward its center. I make it in time to the bathroom, where I heave up nothing but green bile—*how long since I've eaten? Could they be poisoning me?*

I fall onto the bedspread and close my eyes. The last things I remember are the soothing soft sound of the pattering rain- —*there must be a tin roof somewhere nearby*, I think wearily—, a faint scent of coffee, and two voices, one of Serena and one that sounds mechanical.

11

SEPTEMBER 2032
MANY VOICES

I hear a humming sound of many voices. I open my eyes, yet cannot make out where I am, other than I seem to be on my knees with a group of women. There might be men in here, too, although none of the voices is deep. It is so dark in here, wherever we are, that all I can make out are silhouettes. The room flickers with a bit of candlelight.

It's crowded and there is a mustiness to the air, as though people are wearing rain-sodden clothing. Maybe it's raining out. I hear an irregular drip of water. *I hope it doesn't put the candles out,* I think. *They're quite comforting.*

"Amen," someone says and around me there is an answering "amen". I don't want to be found out, so I say, "Amen," too, and the women on either side of me give me little soothing nudges with their shoulders. When we get to a sitting position we are perched on a bench shoulder to shoulder, hip to hip, leg to leg but it feels more— "swaddled" is all I can come up with, instead of oppressive. "Where are we?" I whisper to the women.

"It's safe. We are in the sight of God," one says.

"Can God see us in the dark?" I ask like a child and someone nearby giggles.

"Let's sing," someone says, and to my surprise the women in the room begin singing, "Amazing grace." I was right; there are no low voices. *Not a bass to be found*, I think, and giggle.

"Amazing Grace. That's funny," I say. "That's what they called the waitress--."

"Sh-h-h," someone whispers to me. "Just sing." I stop talking. The soprano and alto voices sound so lovely that I wish I knew the song: "I once was lost/But now am found/ Was blind, but now I see."

"You used to know it," says the woman on my right. "I used to sing it to you."

"And we sang it when I took you to church with me," says the other woman.

"Oh! Are you Serena?"

"Uh huh. Aren't you glad you came with us?"

"Us--who's 'us'? Ashton?" My husband's name starts up a kind of echo in the room, with some of the women chanting, "Ashton. Ashton. Ashton."

"Sh. Ashton's—busy. It's an important night. We need to keep praying for him and the others."

"Who's 'us'?" I repeat.

"Why—the rest of the women, of course. And my mother and your mother."

"*My* mother? *Doris?* Where is she?"

The second push on my right shoulder gives me the answer.

"*Doris?* Doris! I can't see you. Where have you been? Where are we? Are we in a *church?*"

"There are no atheists in foxholes, Caley."

I wish mightily that I could see. It's so dark in here. My eyes are blurry, as though I need glasses. But the warmth of the two women on either side of me is certainly real and satisfying. "Mom," I say, while the singing flows around me, "I am having a strange time."

"Everything will make more sense when our speaker starts."

"Doris—actually I'm afraid to go to sleep. Every time I open my eyes I'm older and I'm somewhere else than I was the night before. . . ."

"Hey, ladies," says a voice that sounds like one I have heard before, "I'm breakin' rules and can't foresee the consequences, God knows, and ain't *that* right?-- and I apologize; but with Caley bein' here an' all, I gotta make sure she's okay, ya know?" All right, maybe she didn't say my name out loud. Maybe I just heard that part in my head, but I recognize the voice: it's the waitress in the diner. What's she doing here in Boston? It's so dark in here, and yet I have a vivid non-visual assurance that our speaker is wearing *purple*.

"Listen up, ladies, we need to leave *right now*. This building has been compromised and is about to be blown up. We'll send word about our next meeting place as soon as possible."

It is so dark! The candles have been extinguished. There seems to be no panic, though. Doris has me securely in one arm and Serena the other. We are feeling our way along to the outside with several dozen others, it seems like, when there is a huge flash of light and an explosive sound. I do not feel the plank dropping with force, the one that lands on my head and knocks me senseless to the ground.

12

JUNE 2042
BANANA BAY

I open my eyes to a familiar sight—Serena's bedroom. *Oh, I know this room!* I think, relieved. There are her two windows, and the fireplace that's never worked—we giggled so many times about having a fireplace in Florida until we decided it was good for just one night a year—Christmas Eve--and the alcove with the window seat and the bookshelves. I've spent overnights with her here so many times. She painted stars on the ceiling once while I held the ladder and we went into laughing fits, so that she dribbled some sparkly paint onto my long blonde hair.

I bring my left hand up to my eyes—no ring. So Ashton never proposed to me. We never married. I dreamed the whole thing. I feel bad about that part, but maybe there's still a chance with him before he leaves town to go to wherever he's going for a year. My heart giving a little pang of already missing him, I hold up my right hand; and there is no little orange tattoo mark showing my marital state—what a fantasy!

Instead, now to my horror there is an "X" over the place where the tattoo would have been—a bright green letter X. My hand has the toughened skin of an older person, not a teenager. I hold up the left hand again and cannot believe that it is also showing signs of age.

Baffled—was Boston a dream? I thought I was in Boston when I closed my eyes! Wait—I also dreamed I was in the dark with Serena and my mother; I can still smell that dank odor in my nostrils. I walk into Serena's bathroom.

But it has been renovated, so much so that I don't recognize it. *Serena!* I think, —*all this time getting yourself a brand-new bathroom and you never mentioned it to me.*

I go to the mirror over what appears to be a plastic sink, although it's a type of material I've never seen before.

"Good morning," says the mirror.

I scream and slide to the floor.

"Good morning. They were wondering when you would wake up. I can order breakfast for you, if you wish."

"Are you—Serena, is this you?"

"I am not Serena, although you are in her bathing room and I was notified several weeks ago to allow you access. I am connected to every room in this house, as well as to the offices of The Royal Pleasantness."

I get carefully to my feet by holding onto the sink. "Well, listen, uh—do you have a name?"

"I am not a person, therefore it is illegal for me to own a name. I own a number. I am not allowed to give it out, except to the person authorized to have it. You are not that person."

"Okay, okay. Well, listen, uh--mirror—I need to know the date. Can you tell me that?"

"Certainly. I am allowed to give out that information. It is June third, 2042. Sunrise was at—"

"No, thanks. Two thousand forty-two. That's—rather startling. Uh—how do I turn you off?"

"Step away from the mirror."

"Uh—can you—*see* me?"

"I cannot. I sense who you are by your breath and the markings on your skin. You are forty-two years old, female, have two sons aged twenty-one and nineteen, not allowed access to Florida. No clear information available concerning them or their father. You are not able to have any more. You have been State married and are now State divorced by permission of The Royal Pleasantness. As such, you are not allowed to re-marry. You have had your gall bladder, uterus, ovaries and appendix Recycled and you will need thyroid surgery in another five point six years if you remain drinking decaffeinated coffee and smoking cigarettes, as the Government doctor has officially warned you. You have type AB-negative blood and you are on the Secondary List to donate in case of hurricane or any other disaster that The Royal Pleasantness deems authentic. You will be promoted to the Primary List after you have been detoxified from abovementioned coffee and cigarettes. You have been advised to wear glasses and cochlear implants."

"Coke--? Wait—I'm *divorced*?"

"Affirmative."

"How do you possibly know that?" But if the mirror knows that I've had my appendix out, then anything is possible. And not able to have any more children--? What's the word they like? Uh--guarantee, information, proof. . . . "Wait. I need proof."

"Proof is the green marking on your right finger."

A woman all at once appears and yanks me away from the mirror. She is—Serena's mother! Oh, I am so glad to see a familiar face!

"Quit talking to that intel source," she hisses, lighting a candle. "You never know what they'll use against you."

"Threat of fire," the mirror cautions.

"It's all right," the woman answers, her mouth a hard line.

"Proof."

The woman pushes her left palm against the mirror, which goes silent. "Ass," the woman mutters as she lights a second candle.

"Oh! I am so *glad* to see you!" I hug Serena's mother hard in my relief.

"Oh, good! *Now* you recognize me. I was so afraid you wouldn't. What's my name?"

"Uh—," Damn, I never called her by her first name. She never was sarcastic with me like this, either. I frown, trying to recall. "Uh—Susan?"

The woman gives a rueful laugh. "Nice try. That's my mother. She's been dead a couple of years now."

I stare. *This—this can't be—*"Serena?"

"Yes—Serena." She narrows her eyes. "You're not going to pull that walking coma routine again, are you? It gets rather tiresome."

What happened to her? She's become so—hard! "No," I say and try to make my voice sound prim and insulted at the idea. "You just—every now and then I think you look like—"

"I look like my mom, I know. A blessing she and my father both died before the age of sixty, although you couldn't be bothered to come to either funeral, thanks a lot for that, by the way. Oh no! Did you order breakfast again? That's extra points—I've already told you that. Really, why do I have a fixing room if you don't use it for meals? And don't spill any water, the way you did yesterday. That's more points, you know. I can't believe you've become so clumsy."

She shakes out a towel that is already hung flawlessly and refolds it. "The mirror didn't tell you that you have arthritis, did it?" I shake my head. "No, thought not. So you can quit using that as an excuse."

"Serena—why are you so cross?" *It can't be me,* I think. *Maybe her looking older is bothering her and she's taking it out on me. Maybe that weight-reducing program she must have been on rebounded somehow.*

"Oh, this is *nothing* compared to how I get every time you show up and disrupt our lives."

"I do that?"

"Look, Caley, this has gotten quite old. I can't keep bailing you out."

"Honest, Serena, I don't know how I got here. Am I—is this your old house in Banana Bay?"

My friend nods. "Well, see, the last thing I remember is being in Boston and you were ordering coffee for us. And then I woke up and we were in the dark, you and my mother and your mother—" She gives a little gasp when I mention her mother.

"Oh, you *are* going to pull that walking coma thing again! Look, honey, you've told me that one so often that you've alienated everybody. The doctors don't want to see you, and we've had the best ones for you. The boys refuse to have anything to do with you anymore. They're—frankly, they're scared of you and the way you have of bouncing in and out of their lives."

The boys—"My sons! The mirror said I have--are they here?"

"Are you crazy? You know they're not allowed in Florida until they're twenty-five. You want them killed?"

"No, of course not! —where's Ashton?"

"He still lives in Boston. It's the only really safe place for him. You *know* that. They live with him and they're both in college there. Don't tell me you forgot that, too. Look, I get so tired of hearing you whine about it."

"We're divorced," I say sadly. I need to go somewhere quiet and think about all this. I need to research what is going on. I need—to be examined by a doctor, specialist, team of them, a psychiatrist--.Except that Serena said. . .

Unless—unless this is all some kind of mind test I'm being put through. But to what end?

Wait. Maybe I'm not the only one. Maybe the Government is experimenting on others, too.

"I need to get out of the house," I say.

"You sure do. About time. You also need to get a job and find your own place. Do you know how strange it is to have Ash come visit me and all the time we're in one end of the house, you're in the room over here, and he and I can't even talk—we have to write notes to each other. We have no idea if you're one of them."

"Them—who?"

"The Royal Pleasantness's Government, of course."

"Why would I be one of them?"

"Because of the Chief of Staff. Because it would be just like you to act dumb, like you've been brainwashed so you can get information."

"Is that what happened? I've been *brainwashed*? Maybe that's the answer! Do *you* believe that?"

"I don't know whether I do or not. It would certainly explain how odd you've become."

"Serena—is there still tv?"

"You know there is—oh God, it's about to go on now."

And as if she had ordered it, the walls and ceiling light up on all sides of the bedroom and canned unctuous organ music fills the air with an amateurish tremolo sugary sound. "Wow! That's *awful--!*" I start to say, when Serena puts a hand over my mouth.

"Shut up. That's The Royal Pleasantness himself playing." I ask her a question with my eyes and she takes her hand away from my lips. "We'll just hope the candle smoke covered your words." She listens intently—for what?

"Don't do or for God's sake say anything stupid," whispers Serena. "You did the last time and Ash almost got in trouble."

"Friends," says a mellow voice, coming from I have no idea where, "be kind. Be true. Be good to one another. Be as The Royal Pleasantness and give yourselves without restraint to all that is good. The Royal Pleasantness wants nothing but good for you. Be peaceful. Tell The Royal Pleasantness."

The words "BE PLEASANT" appear on the walls. "Be pleasant," says Serena, motioning grimly to me that I need to say the same. "Be pleasant," I repeat, looking at her. She points to the walls.

So we talk to the walls, saying the same stupid mantra over and over again until the organ music moves into a diminuendo (*Thank god, I still remember that word from chorus!*) and the pictures fade away—pictures of incandescent blue sky, of rolling waves and translucent waters, of sunbeams and rainbows. I expect chubby little cartoon cherubs and imps to emerge singing from the puffy cumulous clouds.

Actually, I feel better and tell Serena so. "That's the Happy Air they pump into our homes. Don't you dare tell me you didn't know *that.*"

Okay. I am done with querying this hostile woman who looks like her mother, for information. "Is the Banana Bay library still open?"

"Why?" It's not a question of curiosity; one that is more of suspicion, I note.

"I thought—maybe if I read some stuff, newspapers, books—"

"*Newspapers.* If you want archived newspapers, they're in the library basement, although who knows what condition they're in now, the place has been flooded so many times. The library is a propaganda center now, run by the Government. I never go in there because of the lie detectors. Actually, you should stay away from there too. You don't want them finding out anything about your affair with the Chief of Staff. Bad for both of you."

"What?" Huh. So she thinks I had a liaison with another man. That Chief of Staff Somebody. "Was he at least good-looking?" I joke.

"Very. And he wore leather boots. You bragged that he never took them off, even during sex."

Well. I do have a thing for leather. That's something that hasn't changed with age. What a wild joke that must have been and she believed it! What a joke on me—*leather.* "Okay. And—how about a doctor?"

"You know they're all run by the Government, too. You've been to them all. They will not allow you to go through the system again. *And* they don't think you're an interesting case, the way *you* seem to think. What's the matter? Besides your crazy 'comas', I mean."

"I think I might have dementia."

"Don't be foolish. The Royal Pleasantness abolished that as fake years ago. My parents missed it, thank God."

"Serena—how did I get to your home?"

"Oh, now you *are* crazy. Who knows how? You show up every now and then, drunk, swearing like your mom Doris used to do, without bathing in weeks, you reek, and you beg me to take you in—you've lost another job, you're hungry, you're homeless, you're lonely—do I go on? I've heard them all."

"No. Thanks." I am embarrassed, ashamed, confused—is this truly my life? To live like my mother? So that people think I'm some kind of leper? If it's true that I was married to Ashton, then I really need to see him, to have him hold me. Maybe I did something stupid that ended our marriage; if that was so, I can fix it. I *have* to fix it. And I have to see my sons. I'm losing so much time! And should I believe Serena, when she says

I've gotten all the medical help there is? I cannot think she would keep up such a cruel hoax for such a long period of time.

Except I was just in Boston yesterday. An old man in a purple poncho with a Scotty dog was waving to me. No. Wait—there was a dark cavern, maybe, and singers. . .

Out of nowhere I remember a tv show I saw as a kid (of all things, such an inconsequential piece of trivia to remember, proving that my memory has holes in it of being able to retrieve sketchy pieces of the past or not): in this tv show a soldier is brainwashed into thinking he has been in a coma for a long time—but he notices a paper cut on his finger and he knows this just happened a day or two before. It still stings. So he knows they are lying to him.

I rub the green X on my finger. There's a callus on it. It has obviously been there for a while, not just a few days.

"Serena--what do I do? I mean, what job do I have when I have one?"

"Listen, Caley, I'm really over the top with your lies and I'm tired of making excuses for you—it's just one emergency after another with you, one crisis after another."

"You said Ashton comes here."

"Of course he comes here. The Resistance gets him here. We're lovers. You've known that for some time; don't deny it. He's still got that scar on his cheek from when you got desperate and threatened to tell the Government and you jabbed him with a pair of scissors. "

"Oh! I did that?" The idea of my harming my husband—only now he isn't—makes me queasy.

"Caley, I've got to go. I have a lot to do. Just do me one favor—don't try to sell anything of mine. It's all marked and coded and I don't want to have to get you out of detention again. Stupid thing to do anyway, selling what doesn't belong to you." She grabs my right arm and examines my wrist. "Good. Your mother put some more money in your account."

"My mother?" I look at my wrist. There's something like a chip under the skin there.

"Just because you've abandoned her doesn't mean she's left *you* alone."

"I didn't abandon her! I need to find her! Where is she?"

"You know where she is! Better hurry. Don't you dare tell me you forgot she's in the Recycling Center. I'm afraid this may be her day. I've been trying to get that information for you, you know."

I consider. If I'm forty-two years old, that makes Doris --she was forty-two when I was born, so—eighty-four years old. Why, she's an old lady now! I need to see her. Maybe she can make sense of my losing years of my life every time I go to sleep. I have become truly terrified of closing my eyes now.

"But--how is it that she's still working at her age?"

"*She's not working, you dense idiot! She's in line to be Recycled!*" Serena takes a scrap of paper and writes, "They caught her. Ash got away. "

Puzzled, I take her pen and write, "I don't understand."

Chuffing in irritation at what must appear to her to be my stubbornness, she writes, "Underground resistance. Your mother a HERO." She puts it up to my face and as soon as I have read the words she takes the paper to the bathroom, sets fire to it, and places it in the sink.

"Threat of fire," the mirror announces.

"My houseguest was smoking a cigarette," Serena lies.

"Ten points penalty."

"I know, I know." She comes back into the bedroom. "Don't talk," she whispers. "Go see your mother."

14

JUNE 2042
AN INFINITESIMAL CRACK

The Recycling Center, I am told, is actually our old Banana Bay Elementary School. If they're right about no children in Florida, then the schools will be vacant. The streets where I used to ride my bike—it seems like just a few days ago—are silent. The sky, instead of being bright Florida blue, is a dirty hazy color (I've seen photos of Los Angeles smog and that is what the sky overhead reminds me of), so that the sun shining through looks like a metallic discus.

There are only a few people outside and it takes me several moments to realize that all of them are white and are young- to middle-aged adults. I hear no birds. It's a bit of a walk to the beach, but I decide that I will put my feet in the ocean after I see Doris. The silence here is eerie.

There's the church where Serena took me one Sunday. It's a comforting landmark of familiarity, except that there is no cross on top anymore and there's sign inside the glassed-front board where they used to announce the sermon topics: RECYCLING CENTER. But Serena had said that Doris is in our school, so I keep walking.

I look at the windows of homes and am startled when pink and blue lights make the windows glow, all of them. I can hear what I guess is tvs—all of them must be tuned to the same channel—and they are all saying, "Friends," with that sickeningly-sweet organ background music that I heard at Serena's.

A block away I look for the old apartment building where I was a teenager, but it has been torn down and is just an empty space between two newer-built generic-looking homes. I should have expected that it wouldn't last—it had such a forlorn woe-is-me temporary feel to it when we lived there—but it still gives me a sense of sadness, of things gone, lost, the memories plowed down with the building, except for the ones remaining with the occupants. *Don't count my memories*, I think. *Spotty as a Dalmatian.*

As I'm musing about dogs a woman in her forties strolls by with some kind of cell phone, a half-dozen dogs trotting beside her. She has no leashes on them and I want to call out and ask her about that, when two of the friskier ones race up to me, tongues out, looking as though they are smiling at me, floppy ears bouncing. *Cocker spaniels*, I think and I smile out of relief—*doggies!*—now here's something that makes sense.

I wonder if maybe she and I went to school together—she looks about the same age as I might be now; so I stoop down to pet the dogs and I look up at her. "Hey, did you ever--?"

But the woman turns her cell phone toward the spaniels and they jerk back so suddenly it's as if they *are* on tethers. They whine and gasp as though they have been choked; then pad back to her. She has taken no notice of me. I am appalled at her callousness. "Hey, you can't do that!" I call.

She aims her cell phone directly at me. There is not a trace of welcome in her body or her face. Could she hurt me? I have no idea, but it surely seems possible. I halt and she nods as though she has won some game, and walks away, the dogs chastened, not barking even when a scruffy-looking squirrel (*ah! a symbol of a sane world!*) scampers in front of them. It runs up the trunk of an undersized water oak tree and, chattering away, scolds them and me.

It's such a normal sound that it makes me want to weep.

■ ■ ■

I am almost at the school. It used to take me so *long* to get here when I was young, skipping along with Serena. The saplings that were planted when I was attending here have become old oaks that are now dying. I crunch like a child through acorns, dead brown leaves, fallen twigs. I'm almost there; I'm squinting at a street sign (I do *not* need glasses!) and I'm alone except for—there is a flash of purple and it reminds me of something—but what?

"Hey! Wait!" I shout.

A very ancient-looking woman in a bright shiny purple pantsuit emerges from behind a tree. She has obviously been trying to hide. She leans on a cane and appears to be about a century old. "Wait! Come here! I think I know you!"

To my shock, she advances on me as if on oiled roller skates and hits me on the head with her cane.

"Hey!" I'm more taken by surprise than injured, but she continues to batter at me. "Quit it!"

I find I've forgotten how to fight. Well, no wonder--I'm over forty now. Also I know better than to brawl with old people.

Her next blow is below the backs of my knees and buckles me to the ground. Now she is on top of me. I have never known such a strong person, and this gives me the adrenalin rush to overcome my natural reluctance to brawl with someone so obviously decrepit, and yet so hardy.

"Stop it, will you?" I pant, like the dogs I just met. I cannot believe I am a middle-aged woman wrestling with an old lady on the lawn near my old elementary school! Why doesn't anyone notice and come help get her off me?

Now she stares me in the eyes with such a shining, piercing look that I am suddenly afraid this old woman will *kill* me. It's a real possibility. "Help! Help, somebody! Anybody!" I yell.

"Won't do any good. No one can hear you. Sorry I had to flash like that and scare you. There was no time to explain."

"*What?*"

"I just knocked us into an alternate time frame for a few of your earthly minutes, so I can explain things to you."

"*What--?*"

"Don't you know a thing about Einstein and relativity?"

"Old lady, you're not making any--!"

"Look up at the leaves on the trees. Look."

I do, and to my bewilderment, none of them move—they look like a painting, a still life.

"A little blurry, eh? You need glasses, Caley."

"Uh—did you do that?"

"I really didn't, but to your feeble human mind, you *think* I did, and that's all that matters." The old woman gets up and tries to brush some leaves from her dress, but the leaves stay where they are, like the leaves on the trees. "Well, I'll get them later."

I lie on the grass, which I now realize is artificial turf, trying to get my breath back. "Who *are* you?"

"I don't know my name yet. Well, it's not like it might be anything grand and awe-inspiring like 'Gabriel' or 'Michael', say. Those hunks— *pfh.*" She curls her lip. "All messengers and no independent thinking. They're like pizza delivery guys."

"Make sense!"

"Caley--too bad you don't know your Bible. At least you could read parts of it like a novel, even if you won't go to church. Like, you could read St. Paul's letter to Philemon in five minutes—that's an entire chapter, right there. Bam. Done. Jonah's not much longer, with some real twists to it."

"How do you know my name?"

"I gave you a chance just now, see. I was trying to get you to wrestle with me—I mean, I'm strong for a little bit, but then I'm used up. Yep, you could have wrestled with me and demanded a blessing before you'd let me go. That would have done it. Because it's Biblical. I can't get water from a rock, though. Don't ask me that one. And once I tried to part the Atlantic, but all I got was a teensy short dent in the H-two-0 as shallow as if you dipped an oar in while you were rowing. Very disappointing, that."

"What are you *talking* about?"

"I'm saying that you could have held me down for a one-two-three count and demanded something from me. Usually folks want a blessing.

But—I don't know; maybe by wishing to grow up fast you lost your chance."

"Oh, please, no riddles."

"Okay, Caley. I'm going to have to talk in human words to you. Ever read T.S. Eliot and his sexy 'Sweeney Agonistes': 'I gotta use words when I talk to you'? I don't know, I just like that line of poetry. Such a yummy invention, words."

"I know those words! Mr. Mariposa--!"

"Of course you do. Get it? Of *course—high school course*" . . . Play on words, right?" She grins and, for an old lady, shows a startling set of chalk-white teeth.

"*Please. Make. Sense!*"

"Aw. Okay. A couple of days ago according to *your* timeline, you were at Macy's trying on a bathing suit that your mother Doris wouldn't let you buy. You wished to grow up fast and easy and I needed something too, so we just --well, we traded. I know, I know, we're not supposed to trade, but I'd *already* broken a couple of rules, so I thought, well, in for a penny, in for a pound. What's the worst that can happen? Not being able to think like God, of course, I had no idea what would ensue, your honor. I was like an innocent bystander. No, that's not true. I was messing in."

"It *was* a couple of days ago! You're the first one to believe me! So all of this is a dream, even *you*!" I roll on the fake grass and laugh in my relief. "No wonder the sky isn't blue! This is a dream!"

"Yeah, well, as I say—that was all I was gonna do—just knock off four or five years of your growing up and then go find myself something else to do. But I got in trouble, instead."

"What? What do you mean, you got in trouble?"

"Do you have time for a story? That's a joke—of course you do. I've stopped it for you. Time." The old woman seems quite proud of herself.

"You are extremely aggravating, you know that?"

"That's just your menopause talking. Mood swings. Hey. I kept you from all those monthly periods and cramps. The money you saved on supplies! You could at least thank me for that."

"Please. I am *begging* you."

The old woman in purple to my astonishment does a cartwheel, showing unexpectedly that she is wearing purple bloomers. "*Love* doing that. Now. Have you ever heard of the butterfly in the Amazon jungle that beats its wings and changes the course of the planet?"

"Uh—maybe."

"Well, see, I didn't *mean* to—but that's what I apparently did."

"What the hell are you talking about?"

"Okay. Let me try this: ever see the movie "It's a Wonderful Life"?

"Sure. *Oh!* So you're an angel trying to get its wings!"

"Nah. I just like that movie. Now listen. I would say we don't have much time, but we do. Well, *I* do. *You*, not so much. You're already halfway through your life and what have you learned so far?"

"What—is this whole thing a test? A learning experience? I hate tests."

"Well—yes and no."

I swear that if I could grab her cane I would beat her with it, from sheer frustration. As if she can read my mind, she shifts a little away from me. She cranes her neck back, head tilted upward and intones to the clouds, "You see--I very much regret that I stole the opportunity to play God."

The old woman tries to cry, but nothing happens. She scrunches up her face and inhales a few deep breaths, but there are no tears. She winces in disappointment, looks up again to the muddy sky. "Okay, okay! You got me. Can't lie to You. Guess I'm not totally repentant yet."

She turns to me. "Because you see, Caley, actually--I *enjoyed* messing with you and the universe." An old person grin a little like a Hallowe'en pumpkin just beginning to decay lights up her wrinkled face and the wan sunshine points out some chin hairs on her aged jaw. It is not an angelic sight, if that's what she indeed is.

"Uh uh. I'm not an angel, archangel or any of that company of heaven. See, one day *they* were all busy and God needed somebody to go sit on a bus, so She opened up an infinitesimal Crack in the heavens—"

"God is a woman?"

"For your purposes, yeah, She is—'cause I know how not comfortable you are around men. That's also why you see me as female. So as I was sayin', I go sit on this bus—"

"*Real-ly*," I scoff. "A bus. Angels sit on busses."

"You're missin' the point. And I told you I'm *not* an angel. I can read your most recent thought, but that's more like a parlor trick. And now I'm tasked with fixing it—the universe, I mean—well, *your* time in it, which affects the future just like that Amazonian fluttering butterfly—"

She pauses. "Nice words, those. *You* like words, Caley. 'Fluttering butterfly, fluttering butterfly. Hm-m, 'buttering flutterby'—hey, that works, too."

Honestly, I am getting ready to throttle her! But apparently she really can read my intentions and she snaps back to her subject. "Okay, so who says no to God? So I drop down to earth through the Crack and I go sit on this bus next to this nice tired woman named Rosa Parks. I mean, she's had a really hard day of work."

"Rosa Parks? Again—*real-ly*."

"So I'm looking like, for her, like a little old white lady, see, and I give her the message from God: "STAY IN YOUR SEAT." The old woman's voice goes without warning deep and commanding and startles me.

"So? That's it?" I try to sound as though I am disinterested.

She laughs. "God's messages tend to be terse. So-o-o, my ego gets the better of me and I jolly it up a little and put my spin on it and I say to Rosa, 'Honey, you just look plumb exhausted. Now you just keep on sittin' right where you are, you hear? and don't you get yourself up for *nobody*, mind.' So that's what she did." She seems rather smug. "*Lo-ove* to speak Suth'n."

"And now you're here for me."

She grows serious again. "That's just it: no, I'm not. See, I can't leave. While I'm down here God said I might as well deliver one more message—"

"—to me."

"Again, no. You weren't supposed to be in the equation at all. So I delivered my message of encouragement to your old school buddy Owen—"

"Owen! Owen? That nerd?"

"See now, that's where you're wrong. This guy's going to invent some things in the future that will help save the planet. Unlike you, who will continue to just take the easy way through life."

"So what's *he* going to do?"

"He's going to change sea water into drinking water. Actually, we had a laugh about that, how Jesus changed water into wine and Owen's going to change brine into water!" She chortles.

My expression does not change. The old woman folds her arms over her midsection and sighs. "Caley, I don't expect you to understand, any more than that butterfly could, but even so, I'm afraid-- I'm afraid that getting out of your life is above my capabilities. So there, you see, we are."

She shrugs her scrawny shoulders, clucks her tongue and sprawls out on the ground beside me, legs apart as though she is about to make a winter snow angel (which I've always wanted to do). Nobody passes by to catch a rather revolting glimpse of purple bloomers and skinny ankles.

"All beauty's in the eye of the beholder. You *could* have made snow angels while you lived in Boston. I mean you could have remembered that you did, with your two boys. You four all made those cute angels in the snow, but sorry to say that part of your memory's gone. You said you didn't want to live the hard parts of your life, which of course means stuff like childbirth and raising kids and being alone while Ashton was traveling; and when those hard (to you) parts got erased, some good parts did, too, unfortunately. I did tell you I wanted to *play* God, not *be* Her."

Oh, I cannot believe how full of rage I am! I reach out and grab her arm. Her bones feel like chicken wings. "Okay! I demand a blessing. Did you hear me, old lady? I *demand* a blessing!"

She looks past me into the sky again. She seems to be listening for a response. "Uh, no. Afraid not."

"Afraid not *what?*"

"It's not going to happen. You ever see that Superman movie where he slows the rotation of the earth so that Lois Lane won't die? I always thought he was too good-looking for her and I wondered how he could ever kiss her, even if he was Clark Kent, without breaking her face. . . . " The old woman looks away, lost in thought.

"I've seen that movie."

"Yeah, well, that's the comics, not life. So you and I, we're going to have to see this through to the end."

"The *end?* My god! You mean I have to *die?*"

"You *all* have to die, kiddo. But--" and she looks up again as though listening, "instead of a blessing, I can do you a favor. It's what I was supposed to do, anyway. I just let my ego get in the way. I know, I know—we're not supposed to have egos. Want to know how I did it? Got here?"

She actually looks as if she wants to brag. "Sure. What the hell."

"Actually, there's no hell, not the way *you* think of it—fiery flames, pitchfork, et cetera, et cetera."

I sigh. "You know so much about me, then you know I've never been to church."

"Yes, you have. Once. With Serena. You have to be honest with yourself, Caley, if we're going to get through this together."

"How? If I can't remember things? Am I responsible for what I can't remember?"

"It's all your life."

"Okay. So to see hell from your point of view, God. . . ."

"God's *back* is where hell is and you *never ever* get to look into Her face. But *first* you get to look into Her face and it's this glorious all-loving Being who is so absolutely rejoicingly glad you're with Her! I tell you, Caley, there isn't a feeling on your earth that approaches this—well, a very pale equivalent is when you look into the face of your new-born baby.

"Anyway, the truly evil people who die--they won't for some reason receive all that love; they say, "*NO! NO, I WON'T!*" to it—I don't know, maybe they can't face the fact that there's a Power far greater than they pretended to be on earth and they have to keep up the game. So they move away to be in back of Her face. For them, what's written on her brow is 'HONESTY', and they just can't take it. They won't *Face up to it*—that's the right phrase."

"You're making this up, whoever you are." *What if I'm listening to a dangerous crazy lady?* I wonder.

"I promise you I am not dangerous. Anyway, those evil people, they have to keep moving, because they tell themselves they have to stay away from God's face, where all that love is. You ever hear of Jesus saying, 'Get thee behind me, Satan,'? Well, that's it. Get it?"

"If I say 'yes', will you go--?"

"No. I'm still talking. And *you* have absolutely no idea how long 'never' is. So you think *you're* in pain? Pooh. What you're going through is a piece of cake. I am in hell over this. I got no access to the face of God until I make it all right again. And I haven't been *named* yet, because I'm one of a new different kind of messenger that God's experimenting with. Not having a name just tears me apart. What makes it even worse is that while I'm suffering, God is suffering, too."

"That's crazy."

"Your mother suffered right along with you when she had to deny you anything. And that's just the *earthly* kind of suffering."

"She never did."

"Have it your way. And you're not helping us, taking the lazy way through your life."

"Okay. Your philosophical chatter is giving me a headache. I just want to lie here and take a nap."

"No sleeping yet! You have some work to do here and you're not getting out of it that easily."

"All right, Mr. Mariposa. That's who you sound like. *(That's a memory! Oh, that's my memory! Now I remember him-- with his magenta tie! I remember that!)* Continue your lecture. And then—without your help, thanks—I'll figure out how to wake up from this bad dream."

The old woman props herself up on one elbow. "Caley--you know the saying, 'God is everywhere and sees everything'?"

"I've heard it."

"Well, the Crack, the one infinitesimal opening, revealed itself for me to get back—and I didn't. It doesn't stay open all that long." She frowns. "It was foolish, I know. But I was tempted: my ego got in the way, so that I just wanted for one brief instant to know what I would feel like in a purple bathing suit. So I tried to play God, like you people down here do. Only I screwed it up, the same way you guys all do, and I got the purple bathing suit all right, but in this creaky old body."

This time she does a somersault. "Ta-dah!" She seems to be waiting, so I clap my hands briefly. I'm not about to encourage her windbagging much longer.

"I've had plenty of earth time to ponder this, Caley, because, see, since God *never* makes mistakes, then that *Crack* wasn't a mistake; *ergo*, for some reason I was meant to be here; and who knows how many like me squeezed through that Crack, too, and are here trying on their own form of purple bathing suits?"

But I'm not listening to her-- I am so elated! "Yes! Oh my god YES! I remember you now! I remember you! You in your awful bathing suit! Matching toenail polish!" I am so relieved at not having dementia, not being crazy, that nothing else matters at this moment. I really had considered that maybe I was talking to myself, this old lady an imaginary fiction, and maybe I had developed some kind of schizophrenia.

"Caley, I'm trying to tell you—God *is* everywhere! I didn't get away with anything and now I'm paying. Well, I guess you are, too, in a way. And it *will* matter, later."

She hoists herself up by using her cane. "You got a surprise coming your way in an hour. An hour real time, not that wild time ride you're on now, courtesy of me. And I'm not taking all the blame for everything that happened, you know. You're the one wanted to grow up fast."

"Wait! Are you leaving? No, don't go! I need to know more--! I had a husband! I have sons! I don't even know their names!"

"John and Wayne. I'll give you that, too. Remember how Ashton loves those old movies?"

"*Really?* I let him name our sons after a *cowboy actor?*" I am crying with irritation and joy at the same time over this information.

"Can't believe you guessed they were Waiter and Somebody. I laughed myself silly over that one."

"No, wait! Wait! Don't leave! Tell me more! I need to know more!"

"Aha—you're finding out that *life* doesn't wait. Very important lesson learned."

She is gone. Some oak leaves flutter down my body as I scramble to my knees.

A butterfly flits near me and for one brief second settles on my tear-streaked face. The diaphanous brush of the wings feels like an angel's kiss.

15

The pine floor of the old elementary school where I spent my first six years of learning is gritty with sand. There's an old man with a broom at the end of the hall, which I used to think of as endless when I was small, and he's sweeping to no avail, since as I watch him, he tries to pick up some kind of dustpan, but cannot bend over easily, so just scoots the sand under a doorjamb and then continues on.

A robotic machine steps in front of me. "Mission?"

"Uh—to see someone who lives here."

"People do not live here. Name."

"Her name? Doris Marshall."

"Proof."

"Excuse me?"

"Proof."

"Oh—what kind of identification is needed?"

"Proof."

"Uh—search me! I don't know."

So the robot passes a blue beam of light over me and rests on the area where Serena said I had some money from my mother. "Proof."

"Oh no! You need more?"

"Pass." And from the head of the machine a card emerges. I see that the day and year are the same as when I asked the mirror at Serena's, so apparently no large block of time has passed since her house and here. I note the room number on the card and can't believe it—this was my fifth grade classroom, where I first learned to enjoy reading classic books! So they've made apartments out of the classrooms—I find that a delightful idea for retired elders.

The room is upstairs and I stop as the walls are filled with sunshine, the organ music plays and a voice intones, "Friends." I could use some of that Happy Air right now. The old purple lady has left me with a churning bag of emotions. (*John and Wayne—just wait until I kid Ashton about that!*) Also I'm beginning to feel constrained by that damned organ music—like being at a camp where I'm not allowed to just roam around and inspect nature, but have to keep lining up for roll call.

At the top of the worn wide wooden stairs to the second floor is my old fifth grade room where I sat for nine months of the class year next to Serena and we had to be continually reminded to quit giggling; now it contains a dozen or so single beds. There is a very old person in each bed and all look at me eagerly, as though they've never seen a younger woman. Relatively younger. Someone in the room keeps up a steady feeble wailing. Someone else coughs.

They all look alike at this advanced age, the men and women too. Their individual facial features have worn down; their noses and ears have lengthened, with odd tufts of hair growing from those orifices; and their teeth look yellowed and nubby after so many years of use. White heads rise from each pillow on each bed to study me. I can hear labored breathing from some of the occupants. There is an unpleasant stench of urine and mustiness, maybe mothballs. *They sure could use some Happy Air in here*, I think. *Or open a window.*

But those big windows we used to gaze out onto the street from have been boarded shut. The only light in the room comes from the overhead fixtures.

One woman beckons me. She rests in a kind of bolstered-up half-erect position, an extra pillow behind her wispy-haired head. An aging bald man sits, bent over, beside her in one of the few chairs in the room.

"Caley," the woman says. "Caley." A roomful of the elderly mimic dutifully, "Caley. Caley. Caley."

I stare at her. "Are you--Doris?"

"Knew it was you as soon as I saw you. Serena told me you'd be coming. I've been waiting for you. God, I was so afraid you'd be too late! I refused my Calming pill; I wanted to have all my faculties for you." She looks at my hands. "Did Serena give you any candles?"

"Candles? No. Was I supposed to bring some with me?"

"Well. I guess it doesn't matter. We'll just talk softly. You'll have to come closer to this ear, though. I've gone pretty deaf."

The old man rises with some effort and motions for me to sit down on my mother's left side. She nods, points to her left ear. He drags his chair to the other side of the bed. I could assist his labor easily, but my heart goes out at the sight of his looking so proud for doing something physically helpful. My mother takes my hand.

"You came just in time. My Eternity pill will be here in an hour."

"Uh—Eternity pill?"

"The Royal Pleasantness has authorized a way to keep the population from starving. His father, The First Royal, did not believe in global warming, and this Second Royal realized that something had to give; and since the First Royal had outlawed abortion, so that the birth rates started to rise at such an alarming rate, even though bonuses were given to the families of the girls who were willing to Eternalize themselves, and after he said that people could only have two children, *then* he came after us old ones—the ones over sixty. What a crock, telling us that sixty was way over the hill."

(Sixty—I'm forty-two now—I only have eighteen more years to live! I need to see my children! I can't bring to my consciousness having borne them, but my body must remember, must have memories locked inside it.)

"You're not allowed to die of old age?"

"It's been designated anti-Government to be old. The Eternity pill is the absolution and forgiveness to this 'sin'. Crazy, but The Royals believe it. Even The First Royal died that way, as a prime example at sixty, so they told us, although any fool doing the math could grasp that he himself lived into his nineties."

"But look, Doris, I'm forty-two now. That makes you eighty-four. How did you--?"

"I've been in hiding. See all these people? They're *way* over sixty. All of us, we've been in hiding, working for the Resistance. As one of the leaders I tried to find them all safe places, but we're running out of those—funny, no? At my age I'm rather a celebrity around here. And *you'll* have to go into hiding when they find out who you are—you'll be tarred by my brush. Ironic, huh?"

"Hiding?"

"With the Resistance. If it hadn't been for all of his help,—" she motions me closer. There is an odor of unbrushed teeth on her breath and my heart nearly breaks at this lack of being cared for and tended to. "Ashton," she whispers.

"Ash--?" I say loudly as she puts a quivering finger to my mouth and warns me, "Hush."

"Ash," whispers the woman in the next bed. "Ash," cries another, and now a chorus of "Ash! Ash! Ash!" goes around the room. The overhead lights blink like a warning signal and I automatically look toward the door, recalling our fifth grade teacher Mrs. Hornsby standing beside the switch, turning the lights off and on to get our attention and quiet down. The old people in the beds must have had the same upbringing, because they all go silent except for the woman who keeps up her thin wail.

"You see," my mother whispers. "Oh, her. She never got her Calming pill. But she was too scared to tell the robots."

The old man coughs to catch our attention. My mother tells me, "We're going together. When the pills come I'll pretend I've lost mine and they'll give me another. Those robots don't know how to count that well anyway unless it's with a computer and they sure have never been able to understand human sneakiness."

"But--you can't go yet!" Really, this is all incomprehensible—I've just found her and now I'm to lose her! Feelings I thought I never had for her come welling up in me. "I need to know more!"

"You have two beautiful sons, Caley. You should be proud."

"You've seen them?"

"I've *lived* with them, them and their father."

Oh, this is all so unfair! There is not enough time—what has happened to time? "Doris—will it hurt?"

"I've been told it's just like going to sleep. No pain."

"I'm-- I'm afraid to go to sleep, Doris. Every time I do I wake up older and I'm alone and I'm so confused. This is a dream, right?" She shakes her head. "I'm *scared*, Mom." This is the first time I have said any of this out loud and despite myself, I start to cry. For the first time I can remember, I put my head onto her chest and let myself sob. "I've been so alone, Mom. I've been so alone. I'm not—Mom, I'm not liking my life and it's the only one I'm ever going to have! Mom, oh my god, Mom—I guess I've made some awful bargain with an old woman in purple--!"

There's a hand on my back now, big, warm, feeling like Ashton's hand. It's the old man's and he has tears in his eyes, too. He's crooked with age, but I can tell that when he was young he was tall. There is a kindness in his watery look. He circles my shoulders with his arms and leans me against him.

"You don't know me. Why should you?"

My single guess is correct: "You're my Dad."

16

HALF SICK OF SHADOWS

We've had dinner, Serena and I. We've sat through three rounds of The Royal Pleasantness' sappy organ music and "Friends," and are now in the back yard. The absence of stars, tree frogs and night birds is dramatic. Serena has lit candles, has assured the robotic voice that said, "Threat of fire," and has told me, "The candle smoke and scent confuse the messages that the robot machines might pick up."

I've been crying off and on since I got back here and I feel "forworn and forwept", as The Lady of Shalott said. She also said, "I am half sick of shadows." Oh, so am I. So am I.

Now, according to Serena, we are talking in relative safety. "You got to see your father, too."

"A most remarkable man." I've spent most of the afternoon grieving over lost opportunities "So I finally got to meet him on the last day of their lives. Somehow after I was grown they got in touch with each other and were in contact for the rest of their lives."

"Without telling you."

"They said they always wanted to, but they were afraid, hearing of my lifestyle, that I'd be so gullible that I'd accidentally give them away." I am chastened at their judgment of me. Also, I'm irked that I don't remember what my lifestyle has been.

"So what now?"

I have no answer. It all seems so trivial now. "Now it's too late. They had those pills and they seemed content to take them. I wanted to stay— one of the hardest decisions I was about to make, I guess—but they made the decision for me and told me to leave. Something about the robots getting the wrong message."

Serena nods. "Those robots can't figure out human feelings. And they sense that they can't and they're frustrated about this, but of course can't put human emotions into their systems, so the poorer-made ones just burn out their circuits over it."

"My Dad--he begged my forgiveness and I found out about what Mom and Dad had been like before I was born. My mother had had three miscarriages before me—all boys."

"Yes. She had told me." *Huh. Why Serena and not me? Was I not around? Would that have been too hard for me to hear?*

"Right. And Dad was drinking in those days and blaming her and of course she wasn't getting any younger and he was determined that his name should carry on—really such a paternalistic belief--, so he warned her that if she ever got pregnant again, it had better be a healthy boy. If she had a girl, he would leave her. And then—I happened. She said she could see his face through the delivery room window and as soon as I was born and the doctor said, "It's a girl! First baby born in the year 2000!" and everyone was celebrating, he waved at her and just disappeared from our lives."

"I didn't know that part." *Good, I think. Something Doris didn't confide in her instead of me.*

"Yeah, it makes sense now. Being told all this, even at the last minute the way it was, was really pretty freeing—it was as though I was able to go back in my life and see how things had happened. First time I've been able to look *back* in quite a while."

"Caley, just a hunch. Let me see your arm. Yes, I thought so."

The little lump under my wrist where Serena said I had some kind of credit card money is now a different color. "Very smart of Doris—she issued you all of her money before she died. Looks like quite a bit, too. Well, that saves you from having to find a job any time soon. But—it does mean that you can move out."

"What—out of here?"

"Come on, Caley—it's time to grow up. Be on your own. You know how old you are."

"Yeah. Forty-two." I hate to think of myself that way. Inside, I'm still a teenager who doesn't even know how to drive a car or do laundry properly. And I can't keep up with the technology every time I come back! I am now literally in a cold sweat over going to sleep. I haven't told Serena about the old woman in purple who wrestled with me earlier today. For one thing, it sounds crazy, and if Serena thinks so, who knows where I can be placed for "treatment"? Wouldn't I be as apt to be Recycled as an old person?

"Serena. My mother told me about the Age Sixty Law."

"Uh huh. If they can find you. There are plenty of people like my parents were, in hiding. Or they escape Florida for another state where it's less strict. It's hard to get out of here, but there are ways. Lots of water for boats. And the climate's so bad now, there are lots of dark nights."

I think back a couple of days, when I was just out of college and had a wardrobe of purple clothes. Was that some joke the old woman was having at my expense? I can't stand the color and as of today I'm reacting whenever I catch a glimpse of it.

"Did your parents talk at all about—" she lowers her voice, "—the Resistance?"

"Only that Ashton had helped them. Just that."

"Your mother was one of its leaders. She's leaving behind a real gap."

My mother! My mother, whom I thought of as brainless when I was seventeen, thought of as an empty-headed Winston-smoking good-for-nothing! It seems unbelievable. "Yep. She was so revolted when they banned children, people of color and other minorities from Florida, that it fired her up to do all she could for the cause. What? Did you conveniently erase *that* revisionism from your memory?"

Now she looks alarmed. "Oh God. You didn't blab about anything, did you, while you were having that stupid affair with The Royal's Chief of Staff? You could have gotten us all killed!"

"No! Of course not! I would never do that!" *But did I?* My heart sinks. This old class clown could be putting everyone's life in danger out of sheer forgetfulness. And how could my best friend believe -- but now she is looking with narrowed eyes at me.

"I swear to you, Serena, I have never in my life said or done anything against you!"

"Or Ash--?"

I think of the old people more knowledgeable than I, closer to him, saying his name over and over, like some kind of prayer in the Recycling school, "Ash! Ash! Ash!" A spurt of envy hits me.

"No! No, Serena--again, *never!*" *But what if that old purple woman had put humanity at risk by using me somehow as her ego-dummy?* I am sick, thinking that.

"Still. They could have—no, never mind. I've never known you to talk in your sleep. In fact, you're like a corpse when you sleep—dead to the world, not even moving."

"Well, then."

"Look, I'm beat. I really need you out of here tomorrow. Uh—Ashton is coming to stay with me for a few days—"

"Here? He's coming *here?*"

"Sh-h-h. Yes. I wasn't sure if I should tell you because you always make a scene, begging him to take you back. I'm sorry to say this to you, when you're so raw from dealing with your parents' good-bys. But I didn't want his being here to be a surprise, either."

"Ashton--no, no, it's fine. I seem to be learning to deal with a lot of stuff today. That'll just be one more."

But no, no, it's not fine. I need more than anything to see him again. Learning that he is coming here has jolted me.

"I don't want you to hurt him, that's all, Caley. Physically or emotionally."

"Sure. I get it." I look around at my feet. Huh. She's got artificial turf here, too. I'm not sure I've seen any real grass all day. "Hey. Where have the birds gone to?"

Serena sings, "Where have all the flowers gone?" She sighs and hugs me. "Life changes, you know. People change. I'm sorry. I'm really sorry for it all. I'm going to bed. How about you?"

"I think I'll sit up a little longer, thanks." Actually, I'm afraid to fall asleep. I'm afraid life is going to be worse and I'm going to be older and not capable of adjusting. It surely has not been growing better for me. Also: and this is a nagging thought for me—I seem to be more an onlooker in my own life than a participant. I'm missing so much! Well, I'm *not* going to miss Ashton's visit tomorrow. I'll be here for sure. At the least I can apologize to him. At best—who knows? I ache to feel his hands on me, his breath on my face, his mouth on mine, his voice saying my name—yes. All I have to do is stay awake tonight. Just see him tomorrow, dead tired, I don't care. After that I rest.

Serena suddenly laughs. "Remember what you used to do, like Scarlett O'Hara? In Boston. He'd be just home from work, standing at the bottom of the stairs looking up, grinning up at you, and you'd be at the top and you'd call out, "Oh Aya-shton, Aya-shton," in this weird Southern accent, like it was dripping with corn syrup, and then you'd *throw* yourself into his arms and pretend to swoon. That always made the boys scream with laughter."

"Yeah, that was hilarious, all right," I pretend to recall.

"Those were simpler days, except we didn't realize it. Okay, I'll just blow the candles out. Unless you intend to sit here and talk to yourself."

" 'Put out the light; and then put out the light.' "

Serena smiles. "Not going to murder me in my bed, are you?"

"No, no. That's—just thinking about the lights that Mrs. Hornsby used to flick on and off to get us to sit up straight in our seats and stop talking, that's all." A repellent thought has come to me, of going to sleep and waking up older than sixty, in the same bed that was my mother's in the Recycling Center, my life over without my having been aware of it. I shudder.

"Good old Mrs. Hornsby," Serena laughs. "I haven't thought of her in years." She blows out the candles and the back yard is instantly dark. There used to be lightning bugs. Cicadas. Tree frogs.

(Even so, Serena. You've had all those years to remember our teacher, years that you've actually lived. I haven't.)

After she's gone to bed I'll have time to plan for tomorrow. I will not even lie down tonight—I am not going to miss seeing Ashton for anything. And, unlike Scarlett, I *will* get him back. I have to. Oh, I want to reverse course, back to our being in the car heading for Boston! That was only a few days ago!

In the meantime I will stay awake. I need to get on my feet and walk. Walk into the fixing room.

"What are you requiring?"

"Oh! I'd love a pot of tea. Regular, not decaf."

"There is no decaffeinated tea anymore."

"Good. Strong, please."

"It will prevent sleep."

"That's the plan."

I take my brewed tea (it's still a mystery how that's done) to the back yard. There are some searchlights roaming the skies, so that I can make out a wispy cloud of smoke ascending a few blocks away near my old elementary school, but I don't allow myself to consider what is being burned. I sit and sip my tea and look up for any visible stars, but of course with the searchlights, there are none. *I will someday, after I escape tomorrow with Ashton, be an old lady and will tell our great-grandchildren about stars in the sky and the Milky Way,* I think lazily, not even noticing the exact moment when I close my eyes and let drop to the fake turf the teacup with its tracery of tiny purple violets.

17

JUNE 2049
TOBY AND ERNEST

"—I repeat: you were not very wise, coming in broad daylight to visit your mother at the Recycling Center."

I blink. The voice doesn't sound like Ashton's. In fact, it doesn't sound familiar to me at all.

"Oh, you may stall. But we will get the information from you sooner or later, so you may as well make it sooner."

My throat is as dry as if I'd just eaten sand. "Could I have a drink of water, if you don't mind?"

I can't focus my eyes yet; but my nose definitely smells horses. Well, horse dung. I'm not too sure what horses smell like. "They do have those big greeny-yellow teeth, though," I say.

"How much did you give her?" says someone behind me. So there are at least two of them.

"Ten cc's. The usual dose."

"Well, move it to twenty."

"That could be dangerous."

"Nevertheless—we have an order."

Someone puts a glass into my hands of what I am glad to taste is water, my hands which I now discover are bound. Ashton and Serena surely wouldn't do this to me, no matter how mad Ashton might be. "Uh—do you mind telling me who you are and where I am?" I ask.

"No. We ask the questions."

"Well, whoever you are, what you said about my mother was a statement, not a question. So you have yet to *ask* me anything." Now I think I am focusing better and maybe I can make out two men —two short fat men. I am sitting in a chair and I am bound so that I can't fall out of it.

"That ten cc dose is wearing off too fast."

"Well, don't give me anymore! Let me tell you—I must have fallen asleep, although I tried not to—I had tea to keep me awake, but that didn't do it, I guess; and I wake up here in maybe a horse stall, from the odor, with two strangers who want to talk about my mother, whom I had not seen in about twenty years until I saw her yesterday. I could use some information myself, like: what is the date? Where am I? Who are you? And what's *wrong* with seeing my mother, anyway?"

"It is not strong enough and it only makes her garrulous." *Big word*, I think. *Haven't heard that one recently.*

"Have you called The Royal Chief of Staff?"

"He is on his way."

"Well, if he is going to call off this procedure, we had better hurry and have it accomplished before he gets here. Then we can tell him we misunderstood his directives."

"Hey! I can *hear* you! And I can promise you that you're going to be in big trouble when—when that Chief guy shows up."

I expect them to calm down at my words, but instead one says to the other, "Hurry," and a needle is shoved into my arm. "Ow!" I yell. I don't get a chance to recover from that before a helmet of some sort is placed on my head. It has wires attached to it, apparently, because I can feel them draping down my back. Earphones are placed around my ears.

Now I'm scared. Are they, whoever they are, going to electrocute me, just because I visited my mother?

"Your mother Doris Marshall was Elevated by the Recycling Process seven years ago, not yesterday, as you assert."

"You mean she died *seven years* ago?" *Where have I been? Where am I now?*

There is very soothing music being piped into my ears now and I relax, bound as I am, and I feel myself smiling. "So much better than that dreadful organ music that comes from the walls," I murmur.

"Do not say that! You are not allowed to say that about The Royal Pleasantness!" Both men are behind me now and I can hear a ticking clicking sound. "What's that?"

"Nothing to be alarmed about," says one. I hear doors opening and slamming shut from a distance. "Hurry! Hurry!" says the second man.

I think I'll name him Toby. He sounds like he would be a Toby.

"Toby! She said 'Toby'! Look at that on the tape! She is telling the truth now!"

The other one sounds like—I guess Ernest. I feel wonderfully relaxed, as though I am oozing into a puddle of liquid rainbow without any indigo in it.

"Indigo--is that code? What do you think?"

"I think she is either a lot more smart than we thought, or a lot more dumb."

This is so funny that I start laughing. Ernest says, "I told you 10 cc's would do it. We just did not wait long enough."

"We waited long enough!" Doors are slamming and the sound is closer now. "Quick—take that off her head. Remove the glasses from her before he arrives. Destroy that section of tape where she says our names!"

"If he remonstrates, I am blaming it all on you."

"You do, and I will blow the whistle on where you are getting all your extra circuits."

There is silence from the two men. One lifts glasses from my eyes. I wasn't even aware of having them on. No wonder I couldn't see. The ties are removed from my hands and feet and as I stare around, blinking, I realize that I'm in a barn with two—short square *robots*! "Toby and Ernest—I thought you guys weren't allowed to have names," I chide them. This stuff they gave me makes me so humorous!

"Quick! Give her— "

"Too late!" Toby and Ernest, snapping to attention in a mechanical kind of way, both fall silent.

Oh my god. . . in strides one of the most handsome men I have ever seen. I consider Ashton to be very good-looking, but next to this exquisite man with the chiseled features?—well, he's just knocking my socks off! If I took four, no, *five* of the yummiest-looking film stars and blended them, they might maybe come out looking rather like this man. He's tall. He's so well put together. He has just the right amount of a dark three-day beard. And he is wearing leather riding boots. I am such a sucker for leather.

"What did you find?" he demands of the robots, without looking at me. "Sir," says Toby, "she was telling the truth about her mother Doris Marshall. She had not seen her mother since 2017, until Recycling Day in 2042." Actually, if it was not a dream, Doris and I were in the dark some-place together with a bunch of women, but because it was dark and I couldn't actually *see* her, this did not register on their truth meter. I find this hilarious.

"Told ya," I smile in a sappy way, which must be due to whatever they gave me, and not because I am in the presence of this Adonis. Now he looks down at me. "Is she all right?"

"Yes, sir. We have the tape for you to examine, with all the truthful-ness of her life."

"If she mentioned me, she is lying, of course."

"There is no mention of you, sir."

Now Ernest brings out a big roll of what looks like adding machine tape—except that it is a bright purple color. The man stares. "Where did you get this kind of truth tape?"

Toby says, "This is what came from her mind. Her mind is a blank, as the tape shows, and only this purple showed up. She said it might be violet."

"Violet's for rainbows. Purple's for old ladies." I am smiling like a fool and he studies me, one of his perfect eyebrows raised, looking now like the first James Bond. "Wow," I say. "You're gorgeous."

"Sir—"interjects Toby.

"Careful what you say, guys. I know your na-ames," I sing mischie-vously. Think they can tie *me* up and get away with it, eh? Even if they are cute as the dickens.

Now the leathered man snaps into decisiveness: "You two go to the Function room and have your circuits scrubbed." The robots seem to look at me as if wondering if I will tattle.

"Your secrets are safe with me," I say to them. They glide away. I can hear doors close behind them.

"You should not have sent for me by name," the Adonis tells me. "Are you all right?"

"I didn't tell them your name. I didn't know I knew your name. Do I know you?" I ask, rubbing my wrists.

"You were allowed one call and you gave them my name. That was unwise." (*Why is everyone talking about names, for god's sake? And what is his?*)

"I'm still not sure I've ever met you before."

"Ah, good. That is the correct attitude to maintain. Although if the robots questioned you in this sterile room, we can be assured that it is a safe one to talk freely in." He takes a pack of cigarettes from his pocket and offers me one. I shake my head and he lights one for himself. I worry briefly about the combustibility of hay. There seem to be a lot of stacked-up bales in this room. But no horses. This for some reason disappoints me. Maybe what Toby (or Ernest) shot me with is ping-ponging my emotions.

"So—who are you? Have we met before?" I ask.

"I told you—this room is safe. You don't have to pretend now. We can talk here."

"I'd love to. Could you fill me in?" *Look at the sexy way he mouths a cigarette. Look how he holds that long lean sexy body of his, with just the right balance of self-assurance and desire. Oh, I can't take my eyes off him! And I can tell for sure that he is wildly attracted to me!*

"Caley, the only reason I came was because I wanted to be sure you didn't give us away. Having an affair with a Government Chief of Staff is strictly forbidden. I could be sent away from Florida, or worse, if anyone found out."

(I don't get it: which one of us is a Chief of Staff?)

"Did—you and I had an *affair?*" *I can't believe it—I actually saw this great-looking man naked, and I don't remember anything about him!*

"The years haven't been very good to you, have they?" He assesses me coolly.

"*Pity?* I don't need pity from you, mister!" Now I'm offended. I don't think I look that bad. Just yesterday I was looking at myself in a talking mirror at Serena's and wrestling with an old lady and saying good-by to my parents--. "My parents," I say, and my eyes well up with tears.

"Caley—that was seven years ago. You've got to get over it."

Seven years, the same as Toby (or Ernest) said! *Seven years* have gone by since yesterday! That means I am forty-nine years old, and in Recycling terms—oh god, I have just *eleven years to live!* I want to gasp, but this information just makes me smile in a goofy way. Mostly at Leather Boots.

"But the robots said—wait--how old was I when we had an affair?" I demand. Even if we didn't have one, and it may be the effect of the shot I had, I still I want him to take me in his arms, nibble at my ears, rub his leathered legs against my thighs, kiss me until my lips bruise.

Instead he stands firm in those damned enticing boots and considers. "You don't remember? Might be some residue from what the robots gave you. I can tell you—it was 2035. You were a young slim thirty-five years old and so was I. You knew my name back then—you whispered it in my ear enough times. You moaned it enough while we made love. And I don't mean to seem harsh, but apparently the years have been-- kinder to me than to you."

2035. Ashton and I were married in 2022. That meant—I must have had an affair with this man while Ashton and I were married and we had young children! How could I have done anything like that? "I had little boys then!"

"We did not talk about them. You told me you were tired of taking care of everyone and you wanted to be treated like a single woman. You didn't care that I was engaged to another. So we made love, we hid away from others, we took those passionate week ends on Cape Cod--. But. Over. Done with. We swore we would never talk of them again. I take responsibility. I should not have allowed myself to be attracted to you. My position was possibly in jeopardy with The Royal Pleasantness and I was frankly afraid you would turn me over to the authorities, the way you were complaining like a neglected housewife. It had to end."

"But I don't remember any of it!"

"Yes—that is the proper attitude. And it is interesting to see that you put on weight. Good cover. Who would believe now that I ever found you attractive?"

"Oh, yeah—this is a good cover, all right."

"Now—I need to get you out of here and then we go our separate ways. Never speak of this again. Never contact me again. I have risen in the Royal ranks, so that the testimony of any of you women could be detriment--."

"Other women? There were other women?" Now my pride is really stung. I can't believe I was that naïve and stupid when I was married to Ashton. I yearn to see Ash, apologize to him.

"Did we—well, did we have a good time together, at least?"

His lip twists. "Eh-h," he says, making a dismissive gesture with his hand. "You and I possibly could have stayed together longer, but you were --how can I say this—you wanted the easy way out of life. No work. No hard stuff. Rather boring after a while."

Oh, I've had more than enough now. I need to go back to Serena's and soothe my scarred ego. "Well, thank you for getting me out of this--whatever this has been."

"This? Nothing. Happens all the time. Just a clerical mixup, robots getting the wrong information several years too late. Quite a curious thing about that purple paper, though. We've never had anything come from one's mind *purple.*"

I am not over having had my psyche damaged and someone needs to pay for this. "Yeah, well, well—those robots *named* themselves illegally and if you don't take me out for dinner so that I can stare into your face and realize what I've forgotten, then I'll tell everyone their names!"

"Sorry. I am busy. You are old. The robots have already as we speak been Recycled."

Wow. Something Ashton said to me just a few days ago in my time frame resonates: *still a few bugs in the system.* "Also, Caley: I don't know where you have been sleeping and you will pardon me for saying this, but you smell like horse dung."

"That's not *me*! It has to be the horses you have here!"

"There have not been animals in this storage area for at least ten years."

"The bales of hay--?"

"Target practice." Oh. I don't want to ask him anything else, even his name. And I don't want to get into a conversation about where I am staying, because I just don't know where that is.

I must look downcast. He presses a button on some kind of cell phone he has pulled from his pocket. "I am ordering you a car and will call a hotel for you to stay in overnight while you get your bearings. I am not sure what those robots gave you. They mix up doses rather frequently. Don't worry about the costs. It's the least I can do for you. You'll find that the hotel will have—soap."

Then this handsome man gets so close to me that I can smell the expensive cologne he is wearing and he whispers into my ear, "Caley—"

"Yes-s-s?" Oh god, yes. Yes. *Yes!* I look into his beautiful eyes. I could get lost in them.

"Caley, it's Owen. I'm part of the Resistance. I've been able to get a lot of information to Ashton by pretending I'm one of them. I'm counting on you not to give us away."

He stands and raises his voice to a normal level. "It was good to see you again. Don't forget the soap." He slaps a riding crop against his boot and strides away.

That was *Owen?* The same colorblind Owen with the black-framed dorky glasses from high school, the Owen I was told that I took away from Serena once just as a lark? *Owen* turned into that beautiful—that sexy--? I find that more descriptive words fail me.

Damn. I don't know if I feel sorrier for me or for Toby and Ernest.

18

JUNE 2049
A-1-A

The car, I guess, is an American make—"A PLEASANT RIDE" it reads on its grill: not one that was in existence when I was young. I try to climb into the driver's seat, but a warning buzzer goes off: "I am driving this car. Please sit in the rear."

Cowed, feeling a little like Rosa Parks must have, I clamber into the back seat. A spray of perfume mist fills the car. "Do not take this personally. I was ordered to do this by the Chief of Staff."

"Oh." Boy, the insults from Owen just keep mounting. "So this is his car."

"No."

The car heads to the west. "Wait! Where are you going?"

"To the Royal Pleasantness Hotel in West Banana Bay."

"Well—stop and turn around. I want to go to the beach first." It will be so satisfying to walk along the beach and splash through the water!

"Not allowed."

"*What* is not allowed?" Dammit, is that—(better not say his name in front of the car) man going to dictate all my moves? If that injection had any angry juice in it, I'm feeling it now. "I *will* go to the beach."

A taunt from childhood comes back to me and I tell the car, "You're not the boss of me."

To my surprise the car turns east, over the causeway bridge, which is empty of fishermen. They used to be lined up here shoulder to shoulder, I remember (*Yes! I remember this!*). "You can't catch mullet on a line," I remind the car eagerly. I remember that, too! The car does not respond.

To the east, to A-1-A and just beyond that main road, the Atlantic Ocean! The edge of the United States! I want to lean my head out of the (locked, I discover when I bang my head against the clean glass) windows like a dog and inhale the salt air!

Three blocks this side of A-1-A the car stops. "What?"

"Not allowed to go past the marker." Now I look out in front of the car and I see the barricades in the road. "What is it?"

"I do not have that information. I have not been programmed for anything east of the bridge."

"Well, *get* me that information. Unlock my door and let me out so I can see for myself."

"Not allowed."

"Listen, you!—if you do not unlock my door I am going to tell the Chief of Staff that you have given yourself a name, and you will be de-circuited faster than you can—"

There is a satisfying click and I step out onto Banana Bay Beach Drive. I maneuver past the barricades without being stopped. We seem to be the only car and passenger on this side of the bridge, I note. There are no guards here, either. A feeling of being on a deserted isle comes to me.

I walk the three blocks to the beach and stop short—to my horror there is no A-1-A. Instead, immense chunks of asphalt road have been heaved upright and tower over me, and others have caved in before me. It's a picture from a science fiction film and I think momentarily of Charlton Heston discovering the Statue of Liberty.

I clamber carefully among the monolithic shards of road, looking back every now and then to make sure the car is still there and that no guards are appearing out of nowhere to arrest me. There are no familiar sounds of cars, no screaming crying seagulls, no shouts of children on the beach.

It takes a while to move this way. I'm breathing hard from the exertion and the fear that I will fall into what looks like asphalt sinkholes and my hands become raw from the effort. I'm a lemming now, determined to get to the water!

But--there is no beach. No sand. There is at least a twenty-foot drop from where I am balancing to the ocean below. The sound of the waves is a long-remembered song to me, although they are booming against asphalt and concrete chunks of residue, not smooth sand.

I hold onto a narrow piece of metal pipe for support and stare up and down what once was a north-south road. It is now deserted of cars and people: the condos that lined the eastern side of A-1-A have disappeared. There is no sound other than my distressed breathing. What has happened? The Atlantic comes right up underneath where I am standing and I can almost feel it crashing against the carved-out world under my feet. A few seagulls dot the sky in the distance. There appear to be no other living things.

I make my way back to the car. "What happened here?" I ask.

"Please be more specific."

"Where is the beach?"

"I have found information for you: 'In the summer and fall of 2045 there were three hurricanes, one following on the heels of the other, all category three. The substructure of the road named A-1-A collapsed after the Atlantic Ocean moved onto the beach without ever fully receding. Those who were either caught by surprise or who refused to evacuate numbered 29,487 deaths, not counting their pets and some unknown vagrants. The condominiums withstood the first two hurricanes, but the third was too much for them and they all collapsed, having been built on sand.' "

"That's horrible!" I gasp.

"The Royal Pleasantness did not agree. He believed this to be an act of the Resistance and he had 2032 people Eternalized to appease him after there was false information disseminated about global warming."

"My god. Why that odd number 2032?"

It signified the number of years he has been The Royal Pleasantness plus two thousand."

I do some math. Why, then that's the year I was seventeen, when he came into office! "What happened to the President?"

"He was the President until he was appointed by himself as The Royal Pleasantness."

But he was old *then*—he couldn't still be alive! "Is this, like maybe, the Second Royal Pleasantness?" I guess.

"Affirmative. It is the First's son. After that will come the Third, who is two years old now."

"Okay. I've had enough. Let's go to the hotel."

"You said I have a name. I do not have a name." The car sounds almost petulant.

"Yeah, I'm sorry I threatened you with that. You're a good car. Thank you for bringing me here."

■ ■ ■

I've been to better hotels on high school field trips. I remember that. When old Owen Leather Boots said "soap", he really meant it. No nice-smelling shampoo, just a little bar of soap wrapped in paper.

I couldn't do a thing about the clothing I was wearing and resigned myself to putting them back on after I aired them out some. They were generic enough to be a tee shirt and khakis, with mail-order underwear and sneakers-- like something from a dumpster, smelling something like horse.

Here's one thing I really, really miss: I really miss going shopping for clothes!

The hotel manager passed a scanner over me, and apparently my mother had left sufficient money for me, although I made a fuss about having to pay for anything. But since I had no idea how to get in touch with Owen (and I was sure he would deny knowing me if I tried to), I didn't have much of a case.

Here's the worst part: I had the car take me first to Serena's house, and the house is gone! Vanished! It's a vacant lot. So now I have no way of contacting her, or knowing where Ashton is, or our sons John and Wayne, whom I have yet to meet, to the best of my recollection.

I've scrubbed myself as fresh as possible, have wrapped myself in a guest bathrobe (that damned good-looking Owen was painfully correct—I do look rather dumpy), and have ordered dinner from a robot that showed me to my room. "Do you want a tip?" I asked.

"Proof," it said and brought forth a scanner. I let it scan the lump in my wrist that is my mother's money, and I can only trust that the robot didn't clean me out.

There is a tap at my door. I open it to find an old man with a tray and some clothing. "You ordered these," he says.

"I didn't order clothing."

"You will need them. Please dine."

I hold the door ajar. But the old man is not leaving, so I hold out my wrist. "Proof?" I say.

"Oh, Caley, I don't need proof that it's you. How's it goin', kid? Huh—too much light in here," he says, pulling the draperies closed and plopping himself down comfortably in a chair opposite the window.

"Who the hell *are* you?" I demand. In response, he stands up, pretty fast for an old geezer, drops his khakis and shows me—purple drawers.

"Lost all your manners, I see. How you like just whizzin' past the tough stuff in your life so far?"

"How come you're a man now?" This is the most protracted dream I have ever had!

"I keep telling you, it's not a dream. It's your life and I'm stuck in it with you and if we don't get you out of here, you only have, uh, eleven years to live until you're Recycled and Eternalized. We have important stuff to do, but you told me you didn't want to work at anything and that's the rock in the road for me. You're not being allowed to live the hard parts of your life."

"*But I want to now!* I want to see Serena and Ashton and my boys and just be me!"

"Eat your dinner before it gets cold. It smells pretty good, although what do I know, since I don't eat. Serena and Ashton are dead by this point in your life."

"No! What? *How?*" I sit on the bed, stunned. If that's true, then I have no one!

"You have me."

"I don't! I don't *want* you! How did they die? Oh god, this is awful!"

"And yet, because you didn't go through it with them, it's not quite real to you and what you are feeling is not grief or pain, but just hunger pangs and a bit of bruised feelings that I knew something before you did. Both your sons are in prison, but again, because you never knew them, what can you feel except mild jabs of a slight missed opportunity."

"You—you're saying terrible things to me!"

"I am, yes. But you can't really feel them, can you? You know, by the way, that when you say, 'oh god', you say 'God' in small letters."

"*What?*" I am still reeling over the news about my friends and family.

"Yeah. Serena always said 'Oh God' in capital letters, because she knew about Her, but you've only used it as a way to separate your sentences, like, "oh god, it's raining,' or 'oh god, I can't believe what happened to A-1-A', that kind of thing--."

"You could have warned me things were going to change like this!"

"I did. I told you about the butterfly—"

"—in the Amazon, beating its wings, I know, I know! I just don't get it." *Oh god, what will I do now? Everyone is gone from my life!*

"And it's still about you, not them."

"All right, old la—old man, I'm going to bed! See where you get me to next! Maybe I'll go to sleep and I'll be so old that I'll never wake up! How would you like that? What does that do to *your* plans to get back through that Crack?"

I start rocking back and forth. "Oh, Serena! Ashton!" When I am through sobbing I glance over at the old man, who is actually looking back sympathetically at me. I wait for him to tell me something important.

"You know," he muses, "you seem to have made a better mistress than you did a wife. I mean, you liked all those perks, those little trips, the gifts you had to hide from Ashton—pretty exciting, that." He chuckles. "Quite a joke that it was Owen. Even I didn't see that coming."

"Where are they? What happened to my friends?" I ask numbly.

"Well, well. A few years ago you would have been at my throat for that remark I just made. There's progress. And I'll tell you another Einstein idea: matter cannot be created or destroyed."

"They're---not destroyed?"

"You got things to find out yet. I gotta go. I only got this job because I used to be a waitress way back when, about a week ago your time, until I messed with it."

He rises in a surprisingly agile way and he rubs his knees. "You coulda beat me again, Caley. You coulda demanded a blessing from me."

"I want my friends back."

"Don't we all? Don't we all?" I see a flash of purple as he leaves my room. Just then the walls light up, the hateful organ music swells, and the voice intones, "Friends--."

I can't. I can't go on living in this world, without anyone here that I know and care about and who cares for me. I never made many friends in high school, never knew my father except for that brief visit, never got to know my mother as one adult to the other, and I can't remember any people in college—that's blank to me. A purple blank, I laugh angrily, remembering poor Toby and Ernest. *Can't even make long-term friends with robots!*

Suddenly I am furious. I search the walls while I am supposed to be reciting platitudes—"I don't care if you don't approve!" I yell to the uncaring walls. I find the vent where Happy Air is coming in and I stuff it shut. I don't want to be happy tonight!

I sit down at the desk and open its drawers until I find a pen ("this antique pen is the property of the Royal Pleasantness Hotel" is embossed on its flank) and paper.

"To whom it may concern: I am of sound mind. I do not hold the driver responsible." I date the note and sign it "Caley Marshall".

There. I dress in the clothing that the old man left me (he/she even knows my size, which keeps changing over the years), and I feel another surge of fury that he/she knows more about me than I know about myself. There's even a pocket in the khakis for my note. How convenient. How god-damned convenient.

The hotel halls are silent. As far as I know I may be the sole guest here. I hear no cries of babies, no shouts of children, no yaps of dogs, no laughter from any tv sets—none of the homely sounds I grew up with.

I walk quietly outside to the street. There are very few people around and no one talks to me or seems to notice me. No one is casually chatting, I note. The traffic is light, but all it will take is one.

I step into the street casually, as if I am going to cross it. No one notices. A few cars go by, but I'm sure they're driven robotically and would stop before hitting me. What I need is a big truck. An older one and powerful. Heavy with transport.

As if to answer my wish I hear a heavy rumble. I strain to see which way it is coming. Ah, to my side of the road. I have always wondered what I would think, if anything, at the last seconds of my life, and with a deep breath I close my eyes and step into the path of the oncoming truck.

I don't want to connect with his (or her) shocked gaze.

■ ■ ■

My head hurts. I put my hand to it and it feels tender. Am I supposed to *feel* anything when I'm dead? Oh god, maybe I've been dead all along and I can't get any deader! What did the old woman say about hell and not being able to see the face of God? Where's the face, or even the back of the face? Was she lying to me all along? Was I already in hell?

"There's no face of God because you're still alive and good thing, too." I try to sit up. "No, not yet. You have a very nasty bump there. It's gonna hurt for a couple of days—well it *would*, but it *won't*, because you'll be sometime else and it'll be long gone.

"That was dumb, Caley, but I guess I can sort of understand your pain." I open my eyes and there's the old man looking down at me with the same gaze of sympathy that he gave me before I wrote my note.

"Where's the truck? Where's the driver?" I look around for a distraught driver, for a police officer, for skid marks from tire tracks.

"I stopped time. Good thing, too, because you would have killed yourself prematurely. And that would mean you'd be in a dizzying closed loop, just going through the same things over and over again—kind of like a Moebius strip, you know? And just as exasperating."

"What am I going to do?" I moan.

"You're here and I'm here with you for a reason. I'd tell it to you if I knew what it was, but I haven't been given that much insight yet. Now, let's get you back upstairs and to bed."

"I don't want to go to sleep I'm *afraid* to go to sleep. I wish you had a name so I could call you by it."

"Yes, and I also wish I had one. You know these robots, how they name themselves? Just their little way of wanting to be unique? That's why it's against the law for them to have a name, it's such a powerful thing to own. Well, I don't have a name and I'd give anything to have one. That's why we're in this together."

"What does God call you?" I ask, yawning as we enter my hotel room and he helps me into bed.

"Oh now see—that's beautiful. First time you've asked me about God and you even used a capital letter."

"How can you tell?" I want to know, but already the visions of Toby and Ernest and someone in leather are fading from my mind.

"Want a bedtime story?"

"From you? You'd tell a story to me?"

"What a schmutz. Of course. Don't you know the song about fourteen angels guarding you at night? 'Two upon my right hand, two upon my left stand—' "

"That's a lot of angels. Are they like you?"

"They're strong and mighty, like the Hulk. I fear I'm built more like Woody Allen. Ever have a dragon in your bedroom?"

"No. . . "

"Well, who do you think keeps them away?"

"Those fourteen angels."

"Now you're catching on. "

His voice fades out. It's quite odd how I'm all alone, yet never alone. I'll figure that out when I wake up.

Wake up. . . I sit bolt upright. "Oh listen, please, are you still there?" I call out.

"Sure thing, kiddo." I can hear his voice from the chair in the darkened corner of the room.

"I'm—I'm afraid I'll wake up in the same bed in the Recycling Center as my mother—"

"You know she'd done all the work she was supposed to do here. So was she scared?"

"Actually—no," I say, "she wasn't."

"You still have work to do. I know that for sure, even if I don't know what it is."

"You and I could open a diner together. You could be the waitress; or waiter--your choice. . ."

The dark comes in and covers me "from pole to pole" I recall the poem "Invictus" from my readings in high school. "Dark as the night that covers me. . . ."

19

NOVEMBER 2089
TRUTH TO POWER

"YOU CAN'T COME IN HERE!" someone yells.

I hear a collected gasp from a crowd of people and I raise my head. All the people are white and of the same age—maybe thirty to fifty. Hard for me to tell ages, really: they all look alike.

"Lady, you just walked in here like nothing was the matter and you put your head down on a table and we thought maybe you was dead."

" 'Were dead' is the correct usage," I say. " 'Were', not 'was'."

"Lady, listen! We can all get in big trouble if you stay here!"

I look around. One thing I have learned: "Will you please tell me the date? And then I'll leave."

"Tell her quick!" another voice whispers near my ear. Well, it should be "quickly" and not "quick" and apparently somewhere along my life I have had those cochlear implants –uh, implanted—because I heard her voice quite clearly.

"Lady, please—I'm beggin' you. I could get shot on the spot!"

I raise my head and find it is quite painful to do. Well, of course—that bump on my head from the truck near-miss! I move my hands toward my head and am startled to find the skin on them is tissue-thin. I could count the veins beneath the surface; and the skin is pocked with so many dark spots that it seems like freckles.

"Now—what seems to be the problem?" Oh, listen to my voice—it's so quavery, trembly. Me with the voice in high school chorus that was so strong, so sure.

I seem to be in a restaurant of some kind. No, it's a diner. It wouldn't happen to be that same one near our college, would it? "Might I be near Banana Bay College?" I ask.

"Is that where you want to go, dear?" asks a woman. I judge her to be about thirty. She is patting my wrinkled hand as though I am dotty. "I'm afraid that place was torn down years ago." She pulls her hand away from mine and looks around. "You *have* to touch her!," she exclaims. "She feels so different from us!"

Now I see her exchanging glances with other people, apparently patrons of this place. They are all staring at me and they seem to be on edge. It seems to be because of me. Am I bleeding? Naked? What--?

"Maybe she's lost her—you know," says a man about the same age as the woman and pointing to his head. "Maybe someone's had her locked in a cellar all this time."

"Nothing is wrong with my head," I say and my voice continues its quaver.

"Somebody get her a glass of water."

I look around. "Oh, yes, that would be most helpful."

"It's the kind made from the Atlantic Ocean. It's good." I look at the clear water and sniff at it. No odor. I taste it—it *is* good. *Owen did it!* I think in amazement.

I try to get up and find I cannot. "She needs her—what do you call it?--her walker," someone says. "Help her, Joe."

"Yes, please help me, Joe and tell me what the date is and where I am."

"It's November 12, 2089, ma'am. Now will you please leave before we're all shot?"

"Explain, please." I want to say "proof" for some reason and I look at my hands and arms. There is no raised spot where I think money used to be and there's a green X on one finger, a faded X, but still there. I wonder at that: that has to be really good ink.

"Look, lady, I don't know where you came from. You wandered in here just now, sat down at one of my tables and put your head down before I could get you out."

"Why get me out--?"

"You're *old!*" whispers a woman. "Maybe she has, you know, what did they used to call it?" She looks around for help.

"Dementia?" I say. "Wasn't that outlawed by The Royal?" (*How did I remember that?*)

"Dementia, yeah, that's it."

"She sure looks old," says someone else, with a hint of awe. "I've only seen pictures of people this ancient." A man reaches out and feels my hand, then my arm. "Wow," he breathes.

"I am apparently eighty-nine years old," I reply a bit harshly. There is a collective gasp from the patrons. "I actually touched her!" announces someone. "It felt kind of—icky."

Icky. How odd that she said that. Well, I am sure that all words have their own times to fade away and then return. "Unlike people," I muse out loud.

Joe towers over me. "*One*: nobody is that old! And *two*: you got to get the hell out of here! If the Government finds you here they'll think I've been harboring a criminal for years. They won't ask any questions and we'll all be shot, anyone who touched you or talked to you!"

There is a scream, some gasps and curses from those still left in the diner who have been observing me as though I am a dodo bird, and now some people bolt for the door, looking around furtively before leaving.

"Coast's clear," one whispers back before running across the street to a park, where I spot a shiny statue of a man on a horse. Well, I can make that out without glasses. I wonder if I've had eye implants, too, over the years. Actually, I feel pretty spry for my age. But—"How have I survived to this age? Is there no more Recycling?"

"Have you been in hiding?" Joe asks. I guess he is the owner or perhaps the manager. He's at least not shoving me out of the place, although he's clearly terrified of being caught with me in his restaurant.

"You might say that," I tell the few who are still here. "Please," pleads a woman, "tell us where. They've discovered all the old places."

"I regret to tell you that I don't remember. But I will leave, in order to keep you safe." I'm not sure where I will go yet—"Am I in Banana Bay?"—and I receive nods in return. I have to go someplace else, to keep these innocent people out of harm's way.

As soon as I think "innocent people", someone says out loud, "Look! A butterfly!" and points. Over my head flits a gossamer-pale butterfly. "I've never seen one in that shade of purple!" someone else says. "How could that have gotten in here?"

Something is buoying up my heart inside its old bony cage of a carcass. I am feeling *light!* and I don't understand the feeling. I wave to Joe and the others, who carefully wave back. As soon as I am out of the restaurant the curtains are snapped shut.

I make my way across the quiet street, stomping step by step with my walker. I laugh at the memory of an old movie I might have seen just a week or so ago—"The Producers", it was, and I was so young, seeing a—a DVD, that was what it was, with all the old ladies stomping their walkers in time.

And now I am one, too! I marvel. Fortunately the few cars in the road stop for me. The people in the cars stare open-mouthed at me. They are all of them Caucasian and young—maybe thirty to forty years old. Well then, I must be a sight! I must be the oldest person walking around in Banana Bay right this minute! I must look like a dinosaur!

I don't have a mirror to look into, to know that I am aged; but when I turn back, standing in the middle of the street like a traffic cop (*hooray!--a memory from my childhood!*), the restaurant has a big enough front plate glass window that I catch sight of all of me, bent over like—what did they call Hansel and Gretel's witch?—"an old crone". What a picture that conjures up—hunched over, warts on her nose (none on mine, I'm relieved to see), hands like talons. And don't forget the lack of teeth, so that the mouth is caved in and the ancient chin juts way out. A frightening dried-up old hag.

I smile at myself and see that I still have my teeth. Well, there's a blessing. I have somehow managed to powder my cheeks and they are circles of bright pink, which make me laugh. Like a class clown, I am. *And am I wearing lipstick?* I marvel. It appears that way.

Look at my hair! It's shiny white and as long as I wore it as a teenager and the little sunlight there is catches it so that it shines even more. Why, I never fully appreciated how beautiful it is. And what is that on my cadaverous frame? It's a bright purple pantsuit, with a woven shawl to match. *Why, I think admiringly, I look absolutely regal! Lord, I'm so grateful to be alive!*

A butterfly, maybe the same one we just saw, lights on my shoulder for an instant, and I can even feel its tissue weight. *How odd,* I think joyously. *I'm so old and I'm still here!*

I lift one of my feet slightly, enough to note that I am wearing garishly purple canvas sneakers. *What fun!* I think.

There is some kind of parade going on in the park and I am winded by the time I have clomped my way across to the artificial grass. I find to my surprise that I no longer feel afraid, all the way down to my old bones; and when I say out loud, "I'm not afraid!" another butterfly—or perhaps it is the same one—brushes against my saggy face and even gets a bit of my powder from my cheeks on its wings.

If we could hear butterflies, what would they be singing? I wonder. *Are they already singing in a range we can't hear? If they all beat their wings at the same time could they stop the earth in its orbit?* I'm sorry I've never given them enough credit.

It's not a parade. It's a rally of some sort. I sit down on a wooden bench to figure it out and to catch my breath. My hand rubs against the old worn paint of the bench and I feel some indentations, as if from a child's penknife: ASH LOVES CALEY 2020. The tips of my fingers tingle, as if I have just received a gift.

I look casually around and now notice that there are *three* horse statues, with a man astride each one. They must be related, since they all have the same reddish hair and the same superior expressions. *See no evil, hear no evil, speak no evil* goes through my mind. I must admit I am repelled by the statue material, which seems to be some kind of colored Styrofoam and shellac—like old-time surfboards; I revel in remembering that little fact. *Did I ever use a surfboard?* I wonder. Probably not, if it seemed like hard work.

(I wonder why I ever thought that things were hard work, without ever trying them to see if that was the truth.)

The man on a kind of bandstand platform (I remember those!) appears to be quite angry about something. He shouts and waves his arms around and every now and then someone holding a flag hoists it into the air and tips it back and forth. The flag bears huge yellow-green letters the color of algae on a scummy pond: TRP.

Ah: The Royal Pleasantness. Except that the speaker doesn't sound very pleasant.

But the day is more or less sunny, even though it's a muddy-blue sky. My walker works well enough to have gotten me from there to here. I'm warm enough in my lovely shawl, even though the breeze is cool; and nothing on my body is in pain. The bench is comfortable. So it's all good.

There is a sudden hush. I realize that the speaker is staring at me and the people in the crowd, their mouths in large O's, their eyes as huge, has turned to stare at me too. I hear loud groans and gasps from the audience.

"You there!" the speaker points at me. I hesitate. "I said, '*You there!*'"

Now that the people have moved away from the speaker's platform, I see to my shock that this is not a casual gathering: guns are trained on the crowd. The men in charge of the guns look menacing. *These people must have been ordered to be here,* I surmise.

"*Who the hell are you?*" thunders the speaker in a rather high-pitched voice for a man.

"I'm Caley Marshall. Who the hell are *you?*" There is a gasp from the crowd. One of the gunners trains his gun muzzle squarely at me. He is unsmiling. Well, I'm not having that: so I wink at him. Life is too short not to have a sense of humor. I wish I had a flower to stick in the barrel of his gun. I saw pictures of that once.

"*Ha! She asks who I am!*" The young man jeers in what is meant possibly as a joke, except that his eyes don't smile and the crowd laughs carefully with him. "Come up here, old woman!"

"It will take me some time, sir," I respond. "I don't move so fast anymore."

"You will come when I tell you to!" He gestures, and two men from the audience reluctantly pick me up by making a swing with their arms and clasped hands, which I have to say I fully enjoy, hoisting me up to the platform so easily that my sneakers don't touch the ground.

"Whee!" I tell them. "I'm sorry I have to do this," whispers one of the men to me. I notice he is wearing a purple handkerchief in his pocket. I look around and note that all of the crowd, men and women alike, are wearing some kind of purple—a flower, a necklace. . .

"Old decrepit lady! How is it that you don't know who I am?"

"Well, I just got here, I think, and I don't watch tv anymore and I don't read the newspapers—"

The young man's face darkens in anger. "We have no newspapers. Only old people know what the word means. I haven't seen any as ancient as you, not even when I was a boy." He smirks, wrinkling a pimple-spotted nose. "How old *are* you, old lady? You smell like horse dung."

For some forgotten reason this makes me bristle. My age demands some respect! If I haven't earned anything else in my life by taking the easy route, I have at least earned that.

"I am eighty-nine years old and certainly old enough to know my manners. Now I told you who I am and you have not yet returned the favor."

"Arr-gh!" the man screams. "How *dare* you talk to me in that tone of voice?"

He's younger than I first thought, I see. He looks something like the men on the shiny horses. Now that I am (a little too) close to him I can make out that his (shiny also) skin is pasty, as though he has not been outside very often, and his teeth are in bad shape. His forehead and eyebrows are fastened into what looks like a permanent scowl. I would not want to date this man. His only redeeming feature for me is that he is wearing leather boots. But on him? Huh. I find I am no longer attracted to leather. Funny how something—who knows what--can turn one off. . .

"*Who am I?*" he demands of the crowd. "Tell this old crow! Say my name!"

"The Royal Pleasantness!" shouts the captive crowd. He looks down at me and sneers. I guess he's pleased with himself, because he commands that they repeat it two more times and they do, each time a little louder, but without any fervor.

"Well, if you are, then, Your Royal, you have to be over a hundred years old, because I saw you when I was seventeen and you were pretty old at the time."

"You old fool! That was my great-grandfather! And what are you doing here, still alive? Why weren't you Recycled decades ago?"

"Maybe I'm an angel," I say to him. Really, his attitude is bothering me. But it would impolite to just walk away. I couldn't leave that fast, anyway. I look around for my walker and the location of the steps to get down off the grandstand.

"Well, *Carlie* Marshall—"

"Caley," I correct him. His eyes flash confusion for a second. *Maybe he's never been corrected,* I think. *Maybe he's never had good parents or--*

"Well, whoever you are--I have been looking for someone to make an example of—and I believe I have found the perfect person."

Maybe he's never had—maybe he's never had--"I like to think of myself as a good example, sir, but I have to tell you, I haven't been that so much in my life—" I begin, wanting to match my pleasantness to his title.

"Shut the effing hell up!" Spittle erupts from his mouth and to me his eyes look yellow. "You do not talk anymore! Gunners—ready to shoot!" *So I was right—that's what they're called.*

He pulls out what looks like an antique pistol and aims it at me. The strange old-fashioned word *blunderbuss* occurs irrationally to me. In fact, the men in charge of the guns aim them *all* at me. My heart is now beating so fast that I think I may have a heart attack right here on the spot. *Maybe he's never had, unlike me, unlike me--*

"Now, Mr. Royal Pleasantness, I hope I haven't offended you. I'll just leave—"

"I'm bored. You bore me. I've been looking for a little fun and I know what it's to be." He leans down to me and now the grin is lupine and I see in horror that I am receiving a glimpse of evil incarnate. *Oh, you'll only get to see the backside of God,* I think as I watch him rant.

"I'm going to let you leave, old lady. And I'll ensure that nobody does you any harm. In fact, I'll have you set up in a very nice apartment with your own robots—"

"Well. Thank you, Mr. Royal. That's quite generous. I'd like to name them."

"--*or!*-- old lady, I'll just have everyone who has been rounded up off the streets and brought here today shot. As I said, I'm bored. And so are my gunners."

He clicks his gun. "Your choice, Cay-ley." He drawls my name. He makes a motion and his army of men move around so that their weapons are trained on the crowd.

I stare around at their frantic pale faces. Two of the women have fainted. I don't know any of these people, have probably never seen them before, will never see them again. I could live out my days without being afraid that anything bad would happen to me, could die a quiet peaceful death in another ten years or so. Longer. There must be some wonder drugs out there by now.

I could go to sleep right now and wake up some time else, someplace else. I could do that!

"If you think I won't keep my word, I assure you I will. You have my word as the Great-Grandson of The Royal Pleasantness," and now his grin is a rapacious leer. His men shift slightly in their positions, as though to get better aim, not that they could miss at this close range.

But these people are innocent! I think.

"She didn't do anything wrong, except be old," calls out a man near me. I think he is one of the two who helped me up onto the platform. A gunner cocks his trigger. The man falls back into the crowd, his face ashen, his eyes catching mine apologetically. A scared-looking woman pulls at him to be quiet.

"What's it to be, old hag? You still got things to do in your god-awful life?"

But that's just it—I do. I just don't what they are yet. I look around for a flash of purple to help me decide, but there is no sign of any person dressed in purple except myself to tell me that this, like the incident with the truck, is not my time.

"Mr. Royal, let me say something, please. I tried to kill myself yesterday by walking in front of a truck. But that time I had a note in my pocket exonerating the driver; and I have no such note today."

"A truck!" he scoffs. "Where did you ever find a truck in this day and age? So now you're not only ancient, you're also a liar!" He addresses the crowd—"Call her a liar! I command you!"

There is a smattering of words from the audience. The Royal turns back to me, disgusted. "You want a god-damned *note* now? My word's not good enough for you, so you have to have my signature? No! No note!"

"That's not what I mean. And I'm not writing *you* one, either. You're trying to make out that if I say I want to live, that's my decision and if I want *them* to live, that's my decision, but either way: *it's your decision. You* are the one responsible. *This is your act of cowardice, no one else's.* You cannot take the easy way out and you know what?-- I will not, either. And—"(*words come to me from my forgotten past)--*" I am speaking truth to power."

The Royal stares into my eyes and his expression changes, as though he has seen some honesty in them that he cannot bear. I look back into his. I seem to grasp a hint of humanity there, to which I respond in sympathy.

"Why—oh, I'm so sorry! You've never had a *friend*, have you?" I say kindly. What an odd sensation! I feel as though I have just had a glimpse into his desert-like soul. My sorry old quavering voice grows stronger. "I'll bet you've never had anyone ever call you anything but 'Royal'. Let me guess: might your real name be John? Is that it? Or Wayne?"

He grimaces at this. I see a tear and his eyes go large, then harden. All at once there is a roar. I am blown off the grandstand and onto the ground. How did I get *here*? I am confused, am having a hard time breathing. I put my hand to my chest and it comes away sticky with my blood.

There is another sound and this is the one from the crowd. It sounds as though someone just made a touchdown at a football game, the cheering is so overwhelming. "We had Resistance fighters in the crowd," says a woman to me, kneeling and crying. "*You* turned the tide. Someone's gone to get help for you. The Royal is dead and his men are being rounded up. Bless you!"

"Am I dying?" I ask. "I'm not sure it was supposed to be this way."

An emergency technician kneels down beside me and checks me. "Caley, you did it. Total surprise to me after all this-- it was miraculous of you," the EMT says, so low that no one else can hear. But *I* have those cochlear implants, I think crazily. . .

"So this is how I'm supposed to die?"

"No! I never saw this coming! Caley, you did it! I didn't expect this to happen, but what you did was save many people in a self-sacrificing way. You've opened a Crack for me in heaven!"

I try to look up, but all I see is the familiar face of a woman in purple who is smiling lovingly down at me. "You've always been there," I say in wonder. "My God. . .always there. . .."

"In a capital letter. Good for you!" the EMT in purple says, and the sun above me, the sun, oh it's a bright sun again, is shadowed for an instant by—a butterfly flapping its wings.

"I'm going with you then."

"No, Caley. Sorry."

"Oh no!--I've got to see the back of God forever because of my life, is that it?"

"Not at all. You have one more duty to perform."

"How? You said I couldn't go backward, and my forward is about to be used up!"

"Oh, kiddo, you're not going backward or forward."

"You have to quit talking to me in riddles," I gasp.

"Caley. Look up."

I do and there is a magnificent blue sky, whose color I have not seen in decades. I realize it is raining softly on me while the sun is also shining, so that a beautiful rainbow arcs across the sky.

"See that thing up there that looks like a jet contrail?"

"I think so."

"Well, it's not. It's the Crack that I need."

"Wait—will I see you again? What—do you have a name?"

"I do now! You'll recognize it!"

"What—what do I call you?"

"That's just it, kiddo—*you* don't call *me*; *I* call *you!*" She grins at me. "I just gotta do this one more thing!"

She presses her lips against my stomach just below my navel, it feels like. And--she is gone.

For an instant the violet streak of the rainbow glows brighter than the other colors. Now I am aware that people are working on me, putting needles in my arms and pumping my chest rhythmically. It's all very nice, and yet the rainbow is fading and the light is becoming brighter, so bright that I have to close my eyes while the pumping gets harder and I can hear another heartbeat, which keeps sounding more distant.

The light--it's so bright!

20

JANUARY FIRST 2000

"In a flash, at a trumpet crash,
I am all at once what Christ is, since he was what I am, and
This Jack, joke, poor potsherd, patch, matchwood,
immortal diamond,
Is immortal diamond."

Gerard Manley Hopkins

"Sorry to take you away from your New Year's Eve party, Dr. Kelly."

"Hey—for *this* kind of celebration I'm glad to miss all those people sitting around getting drunk. Good thing you caught me before I was one of them, Mrs. Marshall."

"Doc—you know my insides intimately enough that I think it's time you called me Doris. How much longer?"

"You can stop pushing. What time is it, nurse? Have we made it into January first? I can hear lots of whooping and hollering out in the halls."

"It's just a minute into the New Year, Doctor!" comes the answer.

"And here's the New Year baby!" I hear all that, but it sounds a little muffled; and all of a sudden, as though I'm on a rollercoaster, I am whooshed out into the light.

"It's a girl!" I hear someone shout.

"What's the time, nurse?"

"It's 12:01, Doctor! We have the first baby of 2000!"

"A girl! A girl! Oh, I'm so happy about that! Thanks, Doc. Is—is this one—healthy?"

"Never seen a healthier one." I am being rubbed and patted and still can't see anything, so I decide to talk. "Hello!" I say.

But what comes out is a thin "wa-a-ah."

"Look at that—saying hello already. Welcome to the world, baby princess," someone says.

"Now Doris, I hope you've changed your mind about naming your baby after me."

"If it was a boy I thought I would. But she needs a prettier name—no offense, Doc. Kelly—nope, it needs to be-- Caley. With a 'C'."

"Your husband's here," someone says. Then I hear my mother's voice: "Phil! Phil! It's a girl! A girl! Phil--! Oh look, Doc, he's crying, he's so happy."

"That's what new dads do."

"Doris, you hero! All I did was stop for a sec to get a cup of coffee from that machine out there, and look what you did!"

"Phil. What the hell are you wearing? You're not working tonight, patrolling on horseback, are you?"

"You mean my leather riding boots? Funny thing, I had just gotten off duty when your call came. Came as fast as I could. I was getting them all spiffy for Toby, for the parade tomorr—huh. For this morning."

"Toby—huh. That horse doesn't care what you wear. Come on over and give this new Mom a big hug and a kiss."

I am tightly wrapped in something soft and warm and laid on—on my mother's chest! I know it's her—there a familiar smell about her that I would recognize anywhere. Someone has placed some drops in my eyes and I strain to look around. I died—I know I died. Why am I not in heaven? Am I to go through this life again, over and over, with no way out? I don't know if I can do this! If I were not so tired I would feel desolate.

"Good and healthy—look at the way she's scrunching up her face and crying," says someone.

"She's absolutely beautiful."

I feel my fingers being touched and counted, and then my toes. It's actually luxuriant, to be able to lie here and not have to think about anything. I'm exhausted--but I don't dare fall asleep. Where will I wake up next? But my eyelids are so heavy and I can't fight sleep a moment longer. I try to talk, but what comes out is a few feeble wails, and I am falling, falling into the dark, like the dark I just came from.

■ ■ ■

"—and now you're awake. Hello, Caley."

I open my eyes. Today I can see more clearly. I am being rocked by a pleasant-looking old woman in purple scrubs. "Yep, it's me, kiddo."

"What's happened?" I ask, but what comes out is an infant's mewl.

"You got the best gift a person could get—the chance to go around again." She rocks me and smiles down into my face. "I won't be here for long. Got to scoot before the regular nanny comes back. Nice job, rocking newborns in a hospital. You're quite the celebrity, being born at 12:01 am on 01/01/2000. I figured I owed you that, for changing history the way you did."

"I didn't do anything," I said, still making infant sounds, but the old woman seems to understand me.

"Ever hear of P.L. Travers? Ever hear of 'Mary Poppins'? Thought so. Well, she wrote that book, and she also wrote other stories. I'm going to tell you one. You just relax—there's a meaning to it. Yes, you can close your eyes if you want. You other babies, listen up—it's about you, too.

"Travers wrote that this one particular baby was born and she was a little girl who was put into a cradle in her nice proper British home. The sun was shining and a bird appeared on the windowsill of her nursery.

"She found she could talk without words to the bird. 'Bird, I remember where I came from and it was magnificent! Just as soon as I can talk, I'm going to tell everyone about it!' Oh, she was so excited!

"But the bird said, 'You'll forget.'

" 'I'll *never* forget,' the baby girl said, rather offended in the way that only the English can be.

" 'Yes, you will,' said the bird. 'They all do.'

" 'Not me,' pouted the baby, knowing she was talking bird talk that only the bird could understand—what her parents heard from her was a bunch of coos and cries.

"The bird flew away for the winter. In the spring it returned to the same windowsill. 'Have you told everyone?' he asked.

" 'Bah-bah-bah,' said the baby. She no longer understood the bird talk and she no longer remembered where she had come from. The bird nodded his feathery head and flew sadly away, because he knew this would happen, as it had so often before."

I listen: all the infants who had been crying are quiet, so silent that a nurse comes running in to see what the matter is. "They must just like the sound of my voice," says the old woman calmly. "Hey, Caley—your parents are looking through the nursery window at you and making funny faces."

She holds me up carefully, yet firmly, and there stand a man and a woman grinning ear to ear and indeed making funny faces—my mother Doris and my Dad Phil. That's his name: Phil.

"They want to see Caley in the mother's room," says the nurse crisply, grabbing me from the old woman. "Are you sure you work here? I've never seen you before."

"Sh-h-h. I just got them all to sleep," says the old woman. The nurse clucks in disapproval and carries me out of the nursery, down a hall and through a doorway. And there's my mother on a bed and my father sitting beside her, the way I saw them the last time, when I was forty-two years old. It feels as though that was just a few days ago and I'm so glad to see them!

"Look, she's talking to us already!" I need very much to, but all I can get out are baby sounds.

"Okay, Phil, I really want to look her over now that we've got her."

"We get to take her home! We're actually taking our baby home! Can you imagine all the gifts we got, just because of the time she was born? And the photographers! Must not be anything else going on."

"You know this is going on all over the country in every hospital for the year 2000 newborns."

"Yeah, well our Caley has to be the best-looking one."

"Phil—look at this. On her tummy. What do you make of that?"

"Just a birthmark. Nothing to worry about. You know she's been checked over stem to stern."

"It's going to show up if she ever wears a bikini."

"Nah. No kid of mine is going out in public in a bikini. Diapers got more coverage." He laughs. He has such a nice deep voice that I start to laugh. This comes out annoyingly as a cry. *I need to remember that story the old woman told me*, I think, although it's already fading from my newborn memory. I need to remember all I've been through, so I don't make all the same mistakes again. I have to remember!

■ ■ ■

(The bird was correct. Except that every now and then when she caught sight of a flash of purple, her heart would fill with a kind of joy and she wouldn't know why.)

21

I'm at Macy's, looking at myself in their three-way mirror. We've had supper at a kiosk here in the center of the mall, Serena, my mother and I, and I've been so worried that the burger I wolfed down would make my tummy poof out, but it seems to be okay so far. I have tried on a two-piece bikini and to me it looks perfect, gauzy, like gossamer wings—oh, I spin around and look at myself from the rear. I am gorgeous! My body has curves where it's supposed to have curves. I lean over frontwise and there's a cleavage between my boobs. My rear end juts out just enough. Oh, I love it!

"I want to see! Let me see!" Serena comes up behind me. I used to let her borrow my clothes and I would borrow hers, but we've become different sizes this past year, and I know for sure she wouldn't fit into anything this small. "Uh uh. Your mom won't let you wear that out in public," Serena says. Her eyes are round.

"It's my money. I earned it. And it's my body."

At that moment my mother appears behind me. "Nope. You're not wearing that out in public."

"Mo-o-m!"

"It's too skimpy. You'll attract every sailor in town. And you know what I mean."

"It's my money," I say defensively. "I earned it." *You're just jealous*, I think, knowing she wears a huge size ten herself. But I don't say it out loud.

"Will you just look at the price for this tiny bit of material. And size six! You're going to be pulling at your crotch—"

"Mother!"

"It's true. But, if you're determined, we'll give it the acid test." She disappears from the dressing room.

"Wow," breathes Serena. "That was easy. I thought she'd put up more of an argument. What will your dad say? *My* dad wouldn't let me wear anything like this."

"My dad lets me get away with murder," I say. "He's a softy. I can win him over easy." I spend the next minute or so admiring myself. "Serena, I just *have* to get myself a mirror like this one."

"All right. Here we go," says my mother, coming down the hall of the dressing room with a very wide-eyed Ashton. "Okay, young man, just take a look at this. What do you think?"

"I'm in the women's dressing room!"

"Don't worry. Nobody else is in here. One look and out you go."

"Ashton--! Mom, where did you find him? This is so embarrassing!" Never has a boy seen me so—undressed—and Ashton's the only boy in school that I have ever fallen in love with—but I've never told him so. He's a year ahead of me, and about to graduate and go to Europe and I'll never see him again. I feel so naked in front of him!

"So?" says my mother. "Would you be seen on the beach with her?"

"Mom—where in the world did you find him?"

"He and a couple of other guys were heading for that tv and stereo store next door in the mall. That's where they all hang out while their girl-friends are shopping. I just looked around and grabbed one. Why—you all know each other?"

"We all sing together in chorus," Serena says.

"Except we all have more clothes on," says Ashton. He is red-faced and I would feel very sorry for him if I weren't feeling so exposed.

"So, objective observation—what's your opinion? If she was your girl-friend, would you want her out in public with you?"

Ashton is now examining me like a scientist. "I don't know"-- he says slowly. Then he stares at my stomach. "That's an interesting birthmark. Or is it a tattoo? Nope. Like a tiny purple butterfly. Huh." He moves in so close to me that I can smell his shampoo. Oh, I yearn to reach out and stroke his hair. Then I catch my mother's eye. She's having fun! . . .

"Never mind. *Never mind!* I've decided I don't like it enough to buy it."

"Smart move," says my mother.

"I've always thought you would look good in something purple, like that birthmark color."

"Ashton—purple! Yuck—that's for old ladies."

"Well. Hey, you know, I'm starting to enjoy myself." We all laugh. I am moving my hands around, trying to cover myself. He doesn't notice, but my mother seems to be amused. "Is there more of this style show? Serena? How about you? I could sit out there and you two could show me some more—some more bathing suits. I do have an older sister and a younger one. So I know how much females love clothes. What do you say?"

So I try on a few more bathing suits. Serena refuses. We have a good time laughing about them. I end up with a two-piece black one that he says makes me look quite sophisticated. Flattering.

"You gonna pick up the ones you don't want?" my mother asks. I look at the discarded suits in a tired little heap on the dressing room floor.

"Someone will do it. That's what they have saleswomen for, Mom."

"Or I could get that Ashton back in here to come pick them up." I am already scrambling to arrange them on their hangers.

22

JUNE 2017
MARIPOSA

I am just sliding my feet into my sandals and hoping Ashton will still be there by the time I leave the dressing room, although I'm not sure I could face his gaze again so soon—when Serena, eyes wet with tears, out of breath, comes flying in. "Hurry! You have to *hurry*!"

"Who said?"

"Your mother and Ashton are in the tv store. *Hurry!*"

"They're looking at tvs together?" I ask dumbly.

"Dammit, Caley—come on!"

And because she swore and I find this so extraordinary, I race with her through the oddly-empty department store, out into the mall—and I stop. Something unusual has happened. There is absolute silence except for some women who are crying while their toddlers yank at them.

Serena pulls me into the store to stand next to Doris and Ashton, who are staring fixedly at one of the big-screen sets. The picture on all the tvs on all the walls is the same, I see, and the same strange sense of silence, broken only by sobbing (from the women) and blowing of noses (from the men), breaks the stillness of the onlookers.

On the tv screens, however, all seems to be pandemonium. Ashton looks around, sees me, grabs my hand and draws me closer to the sixty-five inch Samsung. My mother gives me a frantic look, her lower lip quivering. It's the way she looked at me when I fell out of a tree once.

"What's happened?"—a couple of people shush me. "The Vice-President is dead."

"Well, this is a lot of fuss"—

"*Watch!*" Ashton is grim. (I have been gabbing while an announcer has been talking as fast as I've ever heard one talk; but then I don't watch the news that often.) So now I pay attention to the announcer, who is stating, his voice breaking, "I repeat: this is a rerun. We'll take you back to the beginning of what we were able to capture."

The words THIS IS A SPECIAL REPORT appear, followed by the word RERUN. A tv camera pans around an immense formal room. There is a huge marble staircase in the center. A commentator's calm voice intones, "We expect the President and the Vice-President, along with their spouses, to pause at the top of the stairway for pictures any moment now. And here they come, for this historic moment."

I see the President, big, beefy, imposing, appear in the left center of the screen as we are seeing it, with the Vice-President a head shorter to his left. At the President's right enters the First Lady, dressed in something long and pale gray. The President wears a white tuxedo, as does the Vice-President's husband. The Vice-President and First Lady have probably huddled together in advance, making sure to wear complementary colors (I wonder absently who got first choice) and now the Vice-President comes forward to stand at the President's left side.

She is wearing a glittering floor-length gown in what I can only describe as a royal purple cap-sleeved, scooped-neck velvet top with a diaphanous skirt of various violet hues; that makes her the only person at the top of the stairs to be dressed in any color and I can't keep my eyes from her, she looks so—beautifully regal. Her husband to her left in his white tuxedo smiles at her the way, I guess, spouses have done since Nancy Reagan gazed adoringly at Ronnie. (I had sat forward during that part of the class film, wondering what she would be wearing and curious about a First Lady who would be interested in horoscopes.)

The President appears flush-faced and furious, but we've all seen him furious before, so nothing is amiss there. The Vice-President looks at him without smiling—("This is curious," says the announcer, "we've never seen her this somber when she's appearing with the President,") and she mouths something we cannot hear.

Without warning the President, his eyes going hard, reaches out with his left hand and *shoves* the Vice-President in the back with such vehement force (we viewers all gasp together in horror, both the onlookers in the actual audience in Washington and those of us at the tv sets in the mall) that she careens, grabbing wildly for the bannister, down the stairs. The sound of her head hitting the marble is truly sickening.

"Poor woman had to be gone before she hit the bottom!" exclaims one of the men near me.

"May God have mercy!" says a woman, sobbing.

The camera stays on the President, thankfully. None of us, I think, want to see that poor woman broken, dead at the foot of the steps. The President's face has set into a grim sort of justified anger—I try to figure out what he looks like; "He looks like he has no sense of remorse!" says Serena, and that is what it is. Several viewers near us nod. No remorse that he has just caused another person's death. There is a white blur at the right side of the screen as the Vice President's husband leaps his way down to his dead wife, calling her name over and over, while Secret Service people rush forward. This is all happening in a few seconds, but it feels to me like hours.

Now we see the First Lady. The President turns slightly toward her. Her mouth is still set in a large O and her eyes are wide. He reaches for her hand and she shakes it away violently, then sinks to the ground in a faint. Someone immediately picks her up and helps her move out of sight of the camera. The President remains alone at the top of the stairs, unmoving, unsmiling.

"Not since both Kennedy assassinations and Dr. Martin Luther King Jr.'s murder have we witnessed anything so --*evil!*" says the announcer, his voice thick with tears. Another announcer chimes in: "The word, Greg, also is 'callous'. What we just witnessed was a cold-blooded act of murder."

"There is no way anyone can put a good spin on this one. I don't—I don't even have words to describe what we are showing you. Please understand that our cameras are not going to show the Vice-President at the bottom of the stairs. Here come the emergency crews, although we can all tell it's too late." Now more people are crying. Some parents have removed their bawling infants from the store, I notice to my relief. Ashton clutches at my hand without seeming to realize he is doing so.

"Bastard!" my mother spits out. "Narcissistic son of a bitch!"

The announcer continues: "We've been able, with the help of some expert lip-readers that we just consulted, to let you know with ninety per cent certainty what the Vice-President was saying in those final moments—" his voice goes thick with tears and he turns away from his desk in front of the camera.

Now they show a closeup of the four people at the top of the stairs—*if we could only rewind life*, I think. Please, I pray silently to the tv technicians, please. Don't make it happen again. I don't think I can stand to see it again and know it's destined to happen.

"Look at those damned flags!" says my mother. At the foot of the stairs are amassed flags with the Nazi swastika and some that look as though they spell out "WHITE SUPREM--". "Look what that man allowed into our nation's House!"

Now there's a closeup of the Vice-President leaning in to the President. She is mouthing words, facing almost forward as she speaks to him. Her words are superimposed on the tv screen: "No. *No.* I told you that I refuse to support you. My lawyers"--. And then there is that horrible shove.

"I vass a child at Auschvitz!" says a very old man in the Washington audience. The tv camera moves to him. We see him as he raises his arm and tattooed numbers appear. "*This* awful man iss not my president!"

Now the flag-bearers look unsure of themselves, where before all this happened they looked triumphant. We see more Secret Service people move toward them.

We have a split screen now, watching that activity, and the other side of screen shows the unmoving face of the President. That look of self-righteous anger remains, along with his famous scowl when things don't go his way. He now smiles and shifts his feet, raising his hands, palms out, fingers up, to speak: "An accident, okay?"--, but he speaks only those three words before the entire Washington audience is shouting, "Murderer! Shame!"

There is a thunderous round of applause from the people in the tv store.

"They're just going to show it again. Come on," Ashton leads Serena and me from the store. "You two can get a ride home with me and my friends. I think your mother's going to be there a while." I look back. She is animatedly talking with other people. "She'd make a good lawyer. I had a great time talking with her while you were getting changed. Before this happened."

My mother? Come on.

"What's next? For him?" Serena asks. We know who she means.

"Trial, although millions of people saw what happened. It's that attitude of thinking the universe revolves around him that's so damned galling. I lay odds that he will plead not guilty."

Now he looks at me. "Once in Mr. Mariposa's class, you said this was all boring and you didn't think one person could make a difference."

"That was light years ago," I answer. We are all sniffling and blowing our noses (something I might not have done once in Ashton's presence, but right now it doesn't seem to matter), walking past crowds of grief-stricken people, united by a man who had made his presidency one of dividing. "She died a hero," Ashton muses. "This changes everything."

"What do you mean?"

"I was just going to have a great carefree time roaming around England and France for a year before college. But this is a wakeup call for me: I need to be interning for the next year at my Dad's law office."

My sense of guilt is like a jab to my throat—it took a death to keep Ashton here. Serena and I exchange a look. We have nothing to add to this.

A tall man in a purple shirt hurries up to us. "They're getting together a candlelight vigil for the Vice-President and her family at Serena's church."

"Mr. Mariposa! I'm in! Come on, Caley, Serena."

I hang back. "What's the matter?" Ashton asks.

"I'm not—will God care if I've never been there?" I blurt out.

"She'll care if you *don't* show up." Our teacher gives me a piercing look.

I stare. "God is a woman?"

"Tonight she is, Caley. Tonight she is." Mr. Mariposa, more frenetic, full of nervous energy than we teenagers are, breaks away and strides ahead of us.

Ashton manages a smile. "Funny guy, huh? But I've learned so much from him." He grabs onto our arms, both to move us along and to keep us from losing each other. The crowd now is growing, a human tidal wave, and in the evening light with the candles, flashlights, cell phones lit and held up into the air (we add to these), the sky looks as though it's full of fireflies. Some people are singing hymns, some are crying; everyone looks shell-shocked with grief.

Serena is crying and now I cry, too, thinking of that beautiful woman in that beautiful gown falling like a flurry of leaves from a tree—I shudder. "I keep seeing her in my head," I say as Ashton squeezes my hand.

"You know," Ashton says, (I think he's trying to get us to think of something else for the moment) "I looked up his name on the internet the other day. The translation of the name, I mean. You'll never guess unless you've taken Spanish." He answers without waiting. " 'Butterfly'. 'Mariposa' means 'butterfly', and that's what the Vice-President's death has done tonight—she's changed the course of history, just like the story of the one flapping its wings in the jungle. Speaking of which. . . "

Mr. Mariposa has turned around and stands as if waiting for us, forcing the crowd to make two paths around him. A tall studious-looking teenaged boy in heavy black-rimmed glasses remains beside him. The teacher nods and points to us.

"Oh no," I say. "It's Owen." (*He'd actually be kind of good-looking, if he'd lose the glasses,* I think. *Huh. Where'd that idea come from?*)

"Go easy on him, Caley. He's really smart. And he's crazy about Serena."

"Nah, she'd never. . ." But now I watch them come together. Owen gives her a hug and they stay that way for a moment before the crowd threatens to separate them. They reach for each other's hand. I find I have a stab of envy. *Of Owen? What a strange night!*

Ashton is talking into my ear over the subdued singing of the crowd. "That Mariposa's sure a unique old bird. I talked to him one day after class to thank him for his insights and he told me how much he loves his job, loves teaching. He seems to know something about *everything.* The way he turned up at our school one day out of nowhere, you would have thought he dropped out of the sky."

We move into Mr. Mariposa's path and he says, as though continuing an interrupted conversation, "Isn't it curious how thoughts will get into your head? I've been musing about this quote of Mr. Thomas Stearns Eliot. Anyone ever read him?"

I nod vigorously. He gives me an understanding look and quotes, " 'Half of the harm that is done in this world is due to people who want to feel important. They don't mean to do harm—but the harm does not interest them. Or they do not see it, or they justify it because they are absorbed in the endless struggle to think well of themselves.' "

" 'And the end of all our exploring/Will be to arrive where we started/ And know the place for the first time.' "

"Why, Caley, you astound me!-- more of Mr. T.S. Eliot!"

"I love to read. I hope books stay around forever." He smiles. "They will now, my dear. Trust me, they will now."

We all must move more slowly as we approach the church. We're caught up in the organic flow of the growing, light-twinkling mass of people. *All of Banana Bay must be out here tonight!* I marvel.

"Hang on, kiddo." Mr. Mariposa's grip feels safe and reassuring and somehow familiar, although I never have held any teacher's hand since kindergarten in my whole entire life and I think I should feel embarrassed, but I don't. Well, I have to be honest—maybe a little.

"Mr. Mariposa," I stammer, "I don't know your first name. Would you tell me?"

"Sure. I have one now! Glad you asked. It's Angelo. Angelo Mariposa."

What a funny thing to say, like he didn't have one before. Well, I'm sure not going to ask him what that means. "Angelo—an angel," I say politely.

"Uh uh, kiddo—not an angel or an archangel or any of the company of heaven. But *close*."

The singing swells louder and sturdier now. How comforting that I am walking with a feeling of expectation up the wide steps and into Serena's church, between Ashton, who just looked down at me and said, "Hang on, Caley. Don't you get away," and Mr. Angelo Mariposa ("I once was blind/ but now I see," the crowd is singing). From the back of the church Mom and Dad join us. Our clasped hands help form a strong human unbreakable chain.

The end-- of the beginning

NOTES

The quotes from T. S. Eliot are from:

1. "Half of the harm. . . well of themselves"—<u>The Cocktail Party</u>
2. "And the end of our exploring. . . know the place for the first time."—<u>Four Quartets</u>.
3. "Sweeney Agonistes" is one of my favorite characters in T.S. Eliot's writings. His "I gotta use words when I talk to you" is from an unfinished poem <u>Fragment of an Agon.</u>
4. The Biblical quote: "Where were you. . . .?" is from the book of Job, chapter 38.
5. I have lost track of where I first read P.L. Travers' short story. It was decades ago and has stayed with me.
6. The short story <u>The Yellow Wallpaper</u> is by Charlotte Perkins Gilman, written in 1892 and based on her life. Some have seen this as the first Feminist piece.
7. The Lady of Shalott could not look directly through windows at life, but could only see the reflection of life through mirrors, which made her "half-sick of shadows".
8. "Amazing Grace" was written by John Newton, 1779. The tune is *New Britain*.
9. "In a flash, at a trumpet crash . . . . " Gerard Manley Hopkins, <u>That Nature is a Heraclitean Fire and of the Comfort of the Resurrection.</u>

I make no apologies for my political point of view. Honesty and truth will always be larger issues than politics, so that makes the larger issue for me in my book, "Where did I come from? Where am I going? What is my mission in life?" I hope, if this book is read in the year 2089, that the reader will be able to say, "What was all *that* about?", since problems of race, religion and supremacy of any kind will be non-existent by then. And, global warming having been pronounced without argument a fact of life, the sun's trying to shine through smog, fossil fuels' burning, the feeding of billions of people and the icebergs' meltings will have been taken seriously.

Barbara Bayley September 2017.

This is Barbara Bayley's sixth book. Her other books are:

"I Could Always be a Waitress" (written under the pseudonym BJ Radcliffe)
"Your End of the Boat is Sinking"   (autobiographical)
"Something to Draw On"
"All Creatures of our G.O.D. and King"
"Hoarding: No Place to Sit Down".

She is still at work, at age 80, as a church organist and music director. She is a retired licensed mental health counselor. She lives in Melbourne, Florida, where she has lived since moving there from Connecticut in 1963. She has three daughters and two sons, eight grandchildren and seven great-grandchildren.